CATA HARI

(Undercover Cat)

D1057179

KAREN COPELAND

Table of Contents

ACKNOWLEDGMENTS

Several people kindly read the manuscript and provided input, including Dr. Ann M. Verrinder Gibbins, John Paul Copeland, and Suzanne Copeland. Thank you very much for your valuable input.

Vanessa Copeland provided many suggestions to help me target the story to the correct age group. This book is dedicated to Vanessa, a true cat lover.

CHAPTER 1

Smokey

Emma Barrett lived in a three-bedroom brick house with her parents and their pets, a dog and cat. The dog arrived three years after Emma was born, but the cat was the most recent arrival. She had been a Christmas gift from her parents after Emma's pleas for a cat had eventually worn them down. The cat had been with them for five years now, Emma thought. Indeed, the cat had quickly made itself at home and now considered Emma's room a retreat, regularly sleeping on the girl's bed, and especially loving to curl up beside her pillow. Emma went to the bathroom to prepare for bed and when she returned, her cat, Smokey, was already in place and fast asleep beside her pillow.

Emma missed her play sessions with Smokey when she got home from school because for some time the cat seemed to be sleeping more often than normal. Her mother had taken Smokey to the vet, but according to him, she was in fine physical condition. Her parents explained to her that Smokey was simply not a very energetic cat, but Emma knew there had to be another reason behind the cat's sleepiness. She was too tired herself to think about it anymore though, and instead she climbed into bed and snuggled under the covers while Smokey purred close to her ear. The poor girl had had a long, hard day at school with a test in mathematics and a surprise quiz in history. She kissed Smokey goodnight, and before long she drifted off into a deep sleep, lulled by the rhythmic sounds of her contented cat.

Contrary to what Emma's parents believed, Smokey was not lazy and certainly did not spend more time sleeping than the average cat. She was in fact a very busy cat with a job that sometimes required her to work during the wee hours of the morning. She had been working off and on for the past two years without her owners' knowledge because her job was top secret. The only one at home who knew that she worked was the family dog. This evening, as she had often done in the past, Smokey was only pretending to snooze, just until Emma fell into a deep sleep. Then she would leave to meet with her boss to get detailed instructions on her next mission.

She continued to purr softly until she was sure Emma was sound asleep, and then waited just a little while longer. Once she was sure that her mistress was sleeping soundly, she rose quietly, as all cats do, and ventured to the edge of the bed. She looked back at her owner to make sure she hadn't disturbed her, and with a swish of her tail she leapt from the bed to the floor. She ran across the room and slipped easily through the partly open bedroom door. As she made her way gracefully down the stairs, she was startled by a loud "harrumph". At the bottom of the stairs a large German shepherd sat waiting for her.

"Cata, do you have another assignment?"

"Yes, Mustafa, I do. I'm meeting my handler tonight down by the docks, but I should be back home before breakfast."

"You be careful down there, Cata. The docks are no place for a lady like yourself, and besides it's not a fit night for cats or dogs out there," Mustafa said with concern.

Keep your voice down," Smokey whispered. "If they hear us talking, we'll both end up as a circus act."

Mustafa was seven years old, and despite the few white hairs that speckled his snout, he looked much younger. In fact, he was a magnificent dog. At times, especially when someone threatened Emma, he could look quite fierce, but most people who met him thought they could melt into his soft, chocolate-brown eyes. He was devoted to his family, and much to their surprise, he was remarkably tolerant of cats. He had accepted Smokey, although grudgingly at first, and they were now the best of friends. When Smokey was tired from a mission, and Emma was still at school, the cat would forego the girl's comfortable bed and instead curl up to sleep with Mustafa.

The German shepherd looked down at the cat named Smokey, but also known by her code name, Cata Hari, and frowned. He worried about her constantly because of her missions. Even though she was very good at her job, she would sometimes get in a situation that only a dog could fix. Like when the security guard trapped her in a sewer and Mustafa had chased him off, then lifted the grate with his teeth to reach her. Then there was the time she almost ended up as dinner for a hungry pack of raccoons. He had chased them off as well because he would never let anything happen to the cat that Emma loved so much. He harrumphed again quietly, as if clearing his throat.

"You listen to me, Cata, you be extra careful tonight, and remember that all you need to do is swish your tail. I'll hear it and come help you."

"I appreciate that Mustafa, but it's probably just a little spying for Max and his group," Cata said as she paced elegantly back and forth in front of the dog. "If I don't leave now, I'll be late, so go to sleep and I'll see you for breakfast."

With a final look at Mustafa, Smokey, aka Cata Hari, escaped quietly through the cat door, and into the foggy night.

CHAPTER 2

Cata Hari's Assignment

The fog was more like pea soup when Cata arrived at the waterfront docks. Although she wasn't fond of the water, she knew how to swim but did it only when she had no other option. What she really disliked was the damp air, and she especially hated the river rats that were ten times the size of any mouse she might choose to chase. She sat on the pier near a large container ship and had only just hoped to herself that her contact would arrive soon, when she heard footsteps in the distance. It was impossible to see who was approaching in the thick fog, so she hid behind a barrel to wait. Before long, a tall man in a trench coat and bowler hat came into view. He was headed in her direction and she stepped from her hiding place to join him.

"Hello, Cata Hari. I apologize for calling you out on such a horrible night, but we have a situation on our hands. I know you'll forgive me when you hear the details," he said.

"That's all right, Max. I rather enjoy the fog, although it is a touch chilly this evening. When do I start on my new assignment?"

"I really would prefer to send one of my human agents on this mission, Cata, because it may be dangerous, but we need someone who can get into smaller places without being noticed. That's right up your alley, isn't it?"

"Absolutely, it sounds perfect for me. Tell me more about the mission."

Max Wolf and Cata walked along the pier until they came to a bench. They sat and discussed the mission and how Cata might help to solve the problem. Max was investigating a case of animal welfare at a research centre and needed an agent who could work without being seen by the security guards and cameras. Max knew that a cat wouldn't be much of a concern for the owners of the building. Even if she were found on the site or caught on a security camera, they would probably let her stay and work as a mouser. However, he knew there were risks to every mission and he warned her to try her very best to keep out of sight. He would hate to see her caught and put in a cage, even for a moment.

"I'm not afraid of that, Max. I can run very fast and jump high as well. But what exactly do you want me to do in the building? I won't be able to protect the animals against the scientists. For that I would need human help, or Mustafa's at the very least."

"Don't worry about that yet, Cata, because what we want you to do is get things on film for us first so we can prove that the scientist who runs the facility is breaking the laws that protect research animals. You see, he was a highly respected scientist who left his position to run this operation. We received an anonymous report about him, but there were no real details provided in the complaint except that the testing done on the animals was not normal. We believe the report to be true, but we must also be careful in case it was made by an unhappy employee, or one who was fired and wants revenge."

Max looked at Cata and he could see that she was, as usual, paying close attention to every word. She was a very smart cat and he knew she was the best agent for the mission. Both Max and Cata turned when they heard whistling further down the pier. A man was coming toward them and they both stopped talking, so as not to attract attention. No one could learn of Cata's ability to speak. Soon a man dressed in laborer's clothes walked past them and boarded one of the ships. Once he was gone, Max leaned in closer to the cat and began speaking again.

"We've investigated this group before, Cata, and everything seemed on the up and up, so we can't approach them again without proof. Also, if they're guilty of something and they know that we're looking into them, they might destroy documents to cover up their wrongdoing. We have to get proof without them knowing what we're up to."

"That's where I come into all of this, right?" Cata asked.

"That's right. I want to fix you with a special camera so you can take pictures while you investigate. It's so small that even your owners won't notice it on your collar. Our main goal here is to make sure that the animals are being treated with respect and kindness."

"I understand, Max, and I can go in tomorrow night to have a look around."

"No, this time you have to go during the day, but a nighttime mission may be required later. I need you to look and listen, Cata. You can learn a lot from watching, but you may learn far more from the discussions between the workers and their boss, a Dr. Ackerman. He's in charge there and you must take care to avoid him, just in case he's up to no good."

"I'll be careful, Max. Let's fix that camera on my collar before I go back home. I'll need a good night's sleep if I'm working tomorrow morning, but remember, I can't start until Emma leaves for school and her parents leave for work."

***

Casper Fox wondered when the company he worked for would be checked out after his complaint. He wished now that he had been more accurate in his complaint, and that he'd been brave enough to give his name. He knew that some of the testing they did on the poor animals was not right because they still used tests that had been banned years ago. What really bothered him though, was the strange behaviour of the man who was in charge, Dr. Ackerman. More than once he had seen the man staring for too long at one calf, and he didn't understand why. Once, he saw him hit the calf, and then continue to watch it, occasionally stopping to write on his clipboard.

Casper pushed his broom along the hallway and was angry with himself. He should have punched Ackerman for picking on a poor animal who couldn't fight back. He stopped sweeping and rested his chin on his hands, letting the broom take his weight.

"I'll keep an eye on Ackerman, and if he touches the calf again, I'll report him. I'll give my name in the report too, even if I do lose my job."

Casper began sweeping again, past the rooms with the dogs, rabbits, pigs, monkeys, and mice, and finally past the room with the calves. He thought about his job and how much he enjoyed working with the animals. In fact, he had loved working there until Ackerman showed up. He didn't trust Ackerman and knew the man was up to something fishy. He decided to keep an even closer eye on all the animals from now on. They were innocent and beautiful creatures who had no one else in the world to look over them, and he decided it was his duty to be the one to protect them.

CHAPTER 3

Cata's Gift of Speech

Max Wolf had been working for the government for most of his adult life. He began as a clerk, doing routine office duties, until one day he found himself in over his head. His boss and all but one of their investigators were away from the office, when wouldn't you know it, that one investigator got into trouble in the field. There was no one available to advise him, and the job came down to poor Max. He was terribly nervous of making a mistake, but he handled the situation like an old pro and found a way to get the investigator out of his predicament. His boss was so impressed that he praised Max's actions to his own superiors and later that year Max entered the training program for government secret agents.

Now he was a senior agent and made a good salary. Max enjoyed his work for the government, and he had a good home life too. He was married and had two grown children in university. He had at least another five years before he retired and knew that when it was time to leave, he would miss his staff, especially Sally Swan who was an agent herself and Max's right-hand person. She was smart and kept Max organized. He hoped that Sally would take over from him when the time came to retire.

If anyone had asked Max what the most interesting event had been in his working career, he wouldn't be able to reveal it to them, but it was indeed discovering Cata Hari. He had been minding his business one day as he ran some errands for his wife. She had asked him to pick up some salmon for dinner while he was out, and he arrived at the store with just that in mind. He was looking at the display of fish in the window of the fish and seafood store when he heard someone speak.

"That is one beautiful trout."

At first, he questioned his hearing, because there was no one standing near him. Then he heard the voice again and looked down to see a cat peering hungrily at the window display, and the cat's mouth was moving. She looked at Max and realized her mistake at once. She hissed, and ran away abruptly, hoping he would be too stunned to follow her. Max was indeed shocked to hear the cat speak, but he soon thought of how valuable a talking animal could be for his investigations. He ran straight into the store to get a take-out order of fish and chips.

It seemed to Max that the search for the cat took a very long time, but the fish and chips were still warm when he saw her tail poking out from behind a tree trunk. He knew it was the talking cat because she was an unusual mixture of greys and her coat reminded him of wisps of smoke. After some coaxing with the fish, he was finally able to sit and talk with her, and they spent an hour together sharing the meal while she told him the story of learning how to speak human, but only after he had promised to keep her secret.

Her great uncle, Zebediah, was the first and the only one she knew of in her family who could speak, besides her own mother, Gabriella. She had told Cata of the amazing antics of Uncle Zebediah. He became a street cat to protect his secret, until he was injured, and then a lonely widow took him in. One day the widow learned quite by accident that her cat could talk, and Zebediah explained to her that human-speak by animals was supposed to be used for good only, and they relied on humans who discovered it to keep it a secret. She swore she would, and they never discussed the subject again. Even after Zebediah passed away, the woman continued to keep his secret.

The first words Cata learned as a kitten were indeed Zebediah and Gabriella, and the rest of the language came to her easily, with her mother's help of course. Unfortunately, she wasn't with her mother long before Gabriella's owner left Cata and her littermates with the Humane Society. She was fortunate that it happened shortly before Christmas, just when Emma's parents were looking for a cat for their daughter. One look at the cat's beautiful coat and they knew she would be perfect for Emma. To Cata's surprise, they took her away from her brothers and sisters to their home, and she was even more surprised to meet a talking dog there. Until then, she had thought that dogs were somewhat stupid and unlikely to speak like her, but Mustafa had an excellent vocabulary and had taught her words she had never heard before. She and Mustafa tried their best to keep their language a secret because they truly loved their family and didn't want to be taken away to be put on display because of their gift of speech. Plus, if truth be told, the two animals cared about each other and were afraid to be separated.

But now Cata knew her speaking skills were not what Max was relying on alone. He needed her understanding of the language to help in the investigation. She knew there would be animals inside the building who could help her in her mission, and in turn, that would give her the ability to help them. She just had to find them. Cata also knew she would have to be careful that none of the humans at the institute learned that animals could speak. Even Max didn't know that speaking was a trait inherited by other types of animals. He thought Cata was the only one, and she wanted to keep him believing just that.

CHAPTER 4

Cata Investigates

Max fitted Cata with her special camera, and then took pity on her. The night had chilled her and she was shivering while he continued with her instructions. He drove her home and advised her to get some sleep when he dropped her off not far from her house. The following day they met again, this time at their regular meeting place in the park, and then Max drove her to the building containing the animal laboratories. Cata had some experience with this type of operation and already knew the best way to get into the building. Plus, Max had told her when there would be deliveries that day. She hid near the loading dock and waited for a truck to pull up to the automatic door of the building, and then quietly slipped in behind the deliveryman.

She had been inside for only a few minutes when she saw the security guard and knew he had seen her too. He was a young, tall, and strong-looking man, and a large ring filled with keys jangled against his hip with each step he took. Cata knew she had two choices, either use evasive action to hide from him, or use her feline ways to win him over. She was surprised when the man approached her first and began talking to her like a baby.

"What a cutie, wootie, pussy cat. Here kitty witty, I have to put you outside."

Cata wound her body around the guard's ankles, rubbed her whiskers against his leg, and then turned large, soulful eyes on him.

"Oh, you poor little thing. It is cold out, isn't it? You can stay for now, I guess. Just don't let anyone else see you."

Cata didn't like to trick this man because he seemed very nice but that was part of her job. She waited for him to continue his rounds before moving on herself. He had just turned the corner into another corridor when she ducked through an open door and found herself in a room of cages filled with dogs. Her fur rose in fear as she expected the dogs, most of them beagles, to start barking up a storm and somehow get out of the cages to chase her. After a few moments though, she saw that the dogs did not react to her at all. They were not only quiet though. Cata thought that the dogs looked sad. She remembered what Max had told her about the experiments on the animals and decided to take a chance that one of them could tell her what was wrong with them.

"Normally you would chase me until I got all the way home. I know you're locked in those cages, but you should at the very least be barking at me. What's going on?"

The dogs stayed in the same positions, lying down in their cages with their snouts between their paws. Some had big, white cones around their heads that prevented them from lying comfortably. Cata stared at them for a while and walked back and forth to get them on film for Max before speaking again.

"What's wrong? Cat got your tongues?"

One of the beagles stared at her and after a few moments said, "Oh really, is that the best you could come up with?"

"I knew one of you had to be able to understand me. I was sent here to find out what's going on. The organization I work for believes that the people here have been hurting you guys. Is that true?"

"Oh yes, they test all kinds of things on us like drugs, household cleaners, and even pesticides. I was bred to serve this way, just like all my friends here. There are at least fifty of us here, maybe more. Sometimes the things they give us make us sick, really sick."

"Why don't they test these things on humans?"

"If I knew that, I wouldn't be stuck in this cage."

"I'm Cata, what's your name?"

"I only have a number, but the nice man who cleans the floor and fills our food and water containers calls me Pumpkin. He sneaks us little treats to eat too, even though he knows it's not allowed. He told me once he'd like to set us all free and that he's waiting for the chance to do it. His name is Casper and he's our only friend. Maybe he can help you out."

"I'll try to find this Casper, Pumpkin, and hopefully we can help to get you guys free."

"I hope to see you again soon then, Cata, and be careful that Dr. Ackerman doesn't find you. He's one nasty guy."

Cata eased her way through the slightly open door, ran to the end of the hall and turned the corner. She was just in time because when she peeked back, a man in coveralls entered the hallway she'd just left. He stopped at the door to the dog room, closed it, and then used a key to lock it. She felt terrible that Pumpkin and his friends were locked up and debated whether to tell Mustafa about the beagles when she saw him next. She decided against it because Mustafa was especially fond of beagles. Plus, although the dog was strong and brave, he was also very soft-hearted and she thought it might make him sad.

Cata almost jumped out of her skin when a very loud screeching came from another open door. She peeked in first, afraid of what was inside, then sneaked in to find a pig in an open pen and tied to the poles of it so he couldn't move. He had a patch of red on his back and he pulled against the ties that restrained him. Between squeals, he heard a meow and he stopped his struggles to stare at Cata.

"I don't know if you can understand me, but please try not to move about because I need to take pictures of you with my camera. It's here on my collar," Cata said.

The pig continued to stare at Cata who had jumped onto one of the rails of the pen to film the mark on the pig's back. Just as quickly she jumped back to the floor and sat down to observe him. The pig observed her right back with intelligent eyes.

"I can speak too you know. My name is Jasper, and I'm a Chester White pig. I come from a long line of Chester's. Unfortunately, I was the runt of the litter and my farmer sold me. Before I knew it, I ended up here where they test chemicals on me. My back is very sore from the last experiment."

"My name is Cata, Jasper, and I'm here to help, but it may take me some time. Right now, I'm collecting evidence for my boss and I hope that what I find out may help to get you released or treated more humanely."

"You're lucky to find me because I'm the only pig that speaks human here, although I heard a rumour that there may be a French-speaking pig in another part of the building. Make sure to be careful of Dr. Ackerman, Cata. He's very unkind and he wouldn't think twice about putting you in a cage."

"I'll be careful, Jasper, and you hang in there. I'll be back when I can."

"Please do come back because I get lonely in here all on my own. I'd love to be back on the farm again and running in the sunshine with the other pigs."

Cata peered around the corner before stepping into the hall. There was no one in sight, but she heard a noise in the distance, a whirring sound. She ran to the end of the hallway and looked around the next corner where a large machine was headed her way. It was leaving wet marks behind on the floor and Cata was afraid it would swallow her up and then spit her out. She ran to the other end of the hallway and found herself once more at the loading dock.

She relied on her inner feline clock and decided that she would not have time to finish her filming in just one day. Max had told her when the next delivery to the building would be, and so she sat and waited for the loading dock doors to open again. While she sat grooming herself, she thought about the experiments they did on the animals. To some people it would seem like routine testing of products, but Cata knew that what was happening had to be against the rules. It was simply cruel to do such things to innocent animals and she would try her best to do something about it. She had to figure out a way to get the animals released and avoid the awful Dr. Ackerman while she did so, but she had no idea yet how it could be done.

Even though Max was in charge, she was still working the case alone, and she had a feeling that she would need help. The animals could only give her their stories so she would need help from Max's other agents, or her best friend, Mustafa. In fact, she felt she would need Mustafa's help more than she ever had before. She would discuss it with him when she got home. The door to the loading dock began its slow opening and she quickly looked both ways to see if anyone was watching and then dashed out when it was just a few inches off the ground.

CHAPTER 5

Cata Reports to Mustafa

Mustafa woke up to find himself on his back with his paws limp above him. He snorted and turned over, disgusted at sleeping that way with no one around to give him a belly rub. He heard a noise and got up to sit by the cat door. He sensed Cata had returned and moments later she slinked quietly through the cat door. Within seconds of her appearance he could smell the scents of the other animals on her and began to sniff her from head to toe, returning to some smells more than once. He followed her to the kitchen and watched as she ate her food and drank daintily from her water bowl. The two animals returned to Mustafa's sentry post near the bottom of the stairs and he laid down, while she snuggled near his chest for warmth. It was not cold in the house, but she was still chilled from what she had seen at the research centre.

"You sure smell interesting, Cata. Anyone would think you'd been working at the zoo. How did your mission go?"

"It was terrible, Mustafa. So many animals in cages and being treated terribly by this scientist called Dr. Ackerman. From what I can tell, one person who works there isn't happy that the animals are suffering and I must find him in case I need his help. All the animals I spoke with warned me about a Dr. Ackerman. I'm going to save them all and make sure Ackerman gets arrested by Max," she said. She got up and moved to Mustafa's tummy and found a more comfortable and even warmer spot. "But I think I'm also going to need your help to pull it off."

Mustafa watched as she nuzzled his stomach, just where he liked his owners to scratch him. "You don't have to do that to butter me up, Cata. You know you can always count on me."

"I'm not doing it for that, I just need to feel close to you after seeing all those animals locked up in their cages."

"Why don't you ask Max to send humans in, Cata? This sounds too much, even for the two of us working together."

"Max wants me to do more investigating first. He's afraid to move in too quickly in case the director there tries to cover things up, destroying records and such. Maybe if things do get tough, Emma can help us."

"She's just a little kid. How can she possibly help?"

"She may be young, but she's very smart. We'll see how it goes, Mustafa, but right now I really need to get a little sleep."

"You nestle up close to me and we'll sleep for a while, until Emma gets home. You need to have some energy when she arrives because she'll get suspicious if you aren't playful. Sweet dreams, Cata."

Cata stretched her back out against Mustafa's stomach and chest. She could feel his heartbeat as she lay there and was reassured by his protection. Soon she drifted into a deep sleep, and even the dog's snores did not wake her.

***

Cata opened one eye, saw the piece of string swing back and forth in front of her, and knew that Emma had returned from school. She was tired, and even a little sore from her adventures that day, but knew she had to play with Emma because she didn't want to be taken to the vet again. She batted at the string with both paws for a while, then rose and wound her body around Emma's ankles, purring the whole time. Emma reached down to pick her up and cradled her in her arms while she sat on the floor next to Mustafa. It was her responsibility to take him for a walk when she got home from school, but first she needed a few minutes with Smokey. Mustafa watched the two of them and wondered what would happen if Emma found out that her cat was a spy. He decided it was too dangerous to even think about it, and instead went to the hallway to get his leash. He carried it proudly between his teeth and laid it before Emma.

"Okay, Smokey, it's time for Mustafa's walk, and when I get home, I have to do homework. Why don't you wait for us in my bedroom and we'll join you when we get back? I'll bring you a cat treat, I promise."

Once the pair had left, Smokey yawned and contemplated going to sleep again. She knew if she went straight upstairs, she'd fall asleep instantly on Emma's soft, comfortable bed. So, she sat at the foot of the stairs and waited for them to return and thought about what to do at the research centre the following day. There were still two hallways that she hadn't investigated, and she didn't know what types of animals she would find. She was afraid of snakes and large birds, but apart from those, she couldn't imagine scary animals being there. Besides, they'll all be in cages anyway, just like today, she thought.

The minutes seemed to go by like seconds as she thought about the mission, and before she knew it, Emma and Mustafa were on the porch outside. She tore up the stairs and pounced elegantly onto Emma's bed to wait for her treat. She hoped it was the tuna flavored one that she liked over all the others. Just the thought made her mouth water.

CHAPTER 6

Cata Meets Anilise

The following day, Cata once more entered the research centre through the loading dock when a delivery was made to the building. She took care that no humans might see her and then headed directly to one of the hallways she had missed on her first visit. She found a cart piled with animal cages and other equipment and squeezed between it and the wall to wait for her chance. This hallway had several rooms with names on the doors and she realized there was only one where animals could be living. Before long, she heard someone approaching, a very pretty woman who was dressed in coveralls and wore a net over her hair. The woman pulled out a key ring to open the door of the one room Cata needed to enter. Cata slipped noiselessly from behind the cart and entered the room behind the woman, running to hide behind a large bag of animal feed so that she would not be seen.

The whole time she worked, the woman chatted in a friendly way with the animals. She had names for them and took each one out of its cage to hold in her arms for a little while before returning them. When she wasn't talking to the animals, she sang softly while she wrote notes on her clipboard. From her spot behind the bag of feed, Cata couldn't see clearly what type of animals were in the cages, but she guessed that they were probably rodents. She watched the woman while she worked and was impressed by how much she seemed to care about the animals. She hoped that there were other workers in the research centre who were as kind.

When the woman left after completing all of her tasks, Cata ventured out slowly from behind the bag of animal feed, looking from side to side first to make sure no other humans were about. The cages were high off the floor and even when she craned her neck, it was impossible to see the animals inside. Then she saw whiskers protruding from one of the cages. She looked around the room and saw something that would help her get a closer look at the animals. She then ran and climbed to the top of a stack of boxes on the other side of the room. From her new height several feet above the floor, Cata looked at the closest cage and could see the pretty, busily twitching nose of a rabbit. The rabbit was not looking her way, so she meowed loudly to get the animal's attention.

"I say, who's there?"

"Don't be frightened, I'm not here to hurt you. Please don't make any noise either because I'm on a secret mission and the humans cannot know that I'm here. Gosh, why do your eyes look all red?"

"Well, my eyes normally are a little on the pink side, but they're red today because Dr. Ackerman has been testing cosmetics on them."

"I thought that type of research on animals was banned years ago," Cata said.

"It was indeed, but Dr. Ackerman doesn't care about rules. He's not a very nice person and he never follows the guidelines for the proper treatment of us research animals. I overheard some of the people who work here discussing how he often breaks the rules and just does whatever he wants," the rabbit said.

"You have the loveliest voice, you know. You sound very sophisticated and intelligent when you speak. Where are you from?" Cata asked.

"I'm a Dutch Belted rabbit, but I was raised in England for research, so I have an accent. The company there went out of business and sold us off cheap to Ackerman. I've always wanted to travel, but not this way. I'm hoping to get out of this research centre someday because I'd like to settle down in the countryside and have a lovely den to raise my future children."

"Would you mind turning your head so that I can see your other eye? You see, I'm working undercover for a government group and I need to get evidence against Dr. Ackerman. I have a camera fixed in my collar so I can take pictures for my boss. Oh yes, that's perfect. Thank you so much. My name is Cata by the way, Cata Hari. What's your name?"

"The animal technician who was just here calls me Anilise. I didn't have a name before that, but I do rather like Anilise, don't you? It rolls off the tongue so beautifully."

"It is a very lovely name. I still have work to do, Anilise, so I must get going now, but I promise I'll be back. Hopefully in a day or two my boss and I will have enough evidence to show that Ackerman is not playing by the rules so that the police can arrest him. Goodbye for now, Anilise."

"Goodbye, Cata Hari. Please don't forget about us."

"I won't forget you. Hang in there, Anilise."

Cata jumped from her perch and stood by the closed door, hoping someone would come into the room so that she could continue on her mission. She heard steps in the hallway through the door, and they slowed to a stop. She darted behind the feed bag again and waited for the door to open. When it did, she saw a man who she thought she recognized from the hallway the day before. He kept his back to her as he swept the floor, speaking gently to the animals as he carried out his chores. While the man's back was still turned, Cata saw her opportunity to escape unnoticed and she ran from the room without making a noise. Once outside, she wasted no time and headed quickly to the next hallway. A sudden screeching from behind one of the doors was so loud that she wanted to run back to the quiet of the rabbit room.

CHAPTER 7

Monkeying Around

Cata had been lucky getting into the rabbit room so easily because the door to the next one was closed, and this time no one was in the hallway to open it. It was obvious there were animals inside the room because all she could hear was loud chattering. After a few moments of listening to the chatter, she looked to see if any humans were about and then dashed to the other end of the hall. There was a small space in the wall containing a water bucket and mop. It was the perfect hiding place, and she squeezed past the bucket to wait, in hopes that someone would come by and open the door. She had become used to the loud noises of the animals in the room she needed to enter. At first, she'd been frightened of going in because of the loud sounds, but now she was eager to find out what type of animals were inside the room.

Before long she heard footsteps further down the hallway and a man's voice singing "You Are My Sunshine". She knew the song very well because Emma sometimes sang it with her mother. She even knew the words and was tempted to sing along but didn't for fear of being discovered.

Suddenly the bucket rattled, and she shrank further back into the darkness of the crevice. When the bucket began to move, she saw the man from the rabbit room roll it away. He was dressed in coveralls, but not like the ones the animal technician with the clipboard wore. His were grubbier and when he stopped to scrub at a spot on the floor, she realized he was a cleaner. As he stooped in the hall, she got a better look at the man. He had a kind face, but she thought he also looked rather sad. He rose from cleaning the spot on the floor and began to saunter down the hall again, rolling the bucket and mop and singing as he went. He stopped outside the room she needed to get into and reached in his pocket for the key to open the door. She left the space in the wall and moved quickly, but quietly, until she stood right behind his feet. He opened the door and propped it open with the bucket, and when he went in to see the animals, Cata slipped into the room and hid behind a stack of boxes.

She watched him as he moved quickly through his chores in the room. He obviously came in here a lot since, judging by how they quieted down, the animals seemed to know and like him. After he gave them food and fresh water, he chatted with each of them in a soothing voice and then began to sing again while he mopped the floor. When he had finished and rolled the bucket out of the room, Cata was alone and a little afraid, but she found her courage and walked slowly toward the cages.

"Ahem," she said, but for her efforts all she got was food pellets thrown in her direction. She dashed away with her ears flattened and hid behind the boxes again. She was not used to being treated so poorly and wondered what she should do next. She didn't know what type of animals they were and was afraid of what they might do to her, but she had to be brave because it was very important that she film all of the animals in the research centre for Max. She took a deep breath and left the safety of the boxes to face them again.

"These ones don't seem to want any help after all. In fact, they are downright mean," she said aloud.

Then she saw movement in one of the cages and a face looked down at her. She knew she had never seen this type of creature before, and thought the animal looked a little like a smaller but hairier human. The animal spoke to her with a lovely, deep voice and she moved closer to the cage to film him.

"Don't say that about me and my friends. We're just frustrated at being locked up day in and day out."

"I'm glad you can talk, and especially glad you aren't throwing your food at me this time," Cata said. "Goodness, what happened to your arm?"

"They tested something on it and put a bandage on afterward. It really hurts. My name is Mac, by the way."

"Lovely to meet you, Mac. What type of animal are you?"

"I'm a monkey. We are closely related to humans, you know."

"I'm a cat, my name is Cata Hari, and I'm trying to find out if the animals here are being treated well. We had a report that you aren't, and now my boss needs proof so he can find out who is hurting you. Have you heard of a Dr. Ackerman?"

"Oh, we all despise him, and make sure you keep your distance from him, my dear, because he is very unkind. Even the people who work for him cannot stand the man. I can't warn you strongly enough to be careful of him, Cata Hari. I swear he was born with a heart of absolute stone."

"No one has said anything good about him yet. So far, I've seen a pig, and some rabbits and dogs. Are there any other types of animals here?"

"You must meet Caruso. He sings so beautifully that I'm sure he could entertain the birds in the trees. He's in a pen in a room near where the scientists have their lunch. You can't miss the lunchroom because there's a big red light above the door. Don't get me talking about food though. Just once, I wish I could have the research centre workers' lunch instead of this awful junk they give us. So, when are you breaking us out of here, Cata Hari?"

"I still have some more research to do today and then I'll see what my boss says. He's very eager to know exactly what's going on at this research centre."

"Some of the people who work here, I think they're mainly students, are very nice. Casper, who was just in here, he's very kind and speaks to us very soothingly. Sometimes he sings too, but he's no Caruso. He might be able to help you in your mission though. But Cata Hari, please make sure that you stay far away from Dr. Ackerman. Don't fall for any of his monkey business."

Both Mac and Cata laughed at the joke he'd made. She was surprised that the poor monkey could find a sense of humor to share with her when his arm hurt so.

"I really like you, Mac. Thank you for telling me about Caruso. I'll check in on him next, and then I think I'll have enough to report back to my supervisor, at least for this part of my mission. You hang in there, Mac, and I hope your arm feels better soon."

Cata was about to turn around to wait by the door to the room when it opened suddenly. She thought someone was going to come into the room, but although they had obviously meant to, they changed their mind at the last moment. The door was on a spring and it began to close slowly, giving the cat just enough time to escape into the hall. She dashed to the space with the mop and bucket and settled in behind. She wanted to have a think about what she'd learned so far, and then she would have a brief nap before heading back out to find Caruso.

CHAPTER 8

Cata Meets the Singing Steer

Cata woke from her nap and her inner clock told her that she still had time for more investigating before meeting with Max for an update, and to exchange her camera for a new one for the following day. She peeked around the bucket and saw no one coming, so she ran to the other end of the hallway. If she could find the lunchroom, she knew she'd be able to find Caruso, and the first part of her mission would be complete. She heard voices and stopped momentarily before looking carefully around the next corner.

People were entering a room with bags. She could smell the food from where she waited and knew she had found the lunchroom that Mac had mentioned. When the coast was clear, she made a dash past the lunchroom and ducked through the first open door she found. It was full of large cages with open tops and inside each was a black and white animal. She knew from drives in the country with her family that they were called Holsteins. They all looked at her and she said, "Do any of you speak?" None of them replied, but several bellowed loudly. She jumped at the noise they made and wanted to run from the room, but remained a while longer, just in case one of them answered. After a few moments, she got up and turned to leave, but stopped when she heard a lovely, rich voice. She didn't know a lot about music but recognized the tune from one of the opera tapes that Emma's mother sometimes played. When the calf stopped singing, he signaled to her with his snout.

"Pssst, hey cat, I can talk like you, and I need to get out of here as soon as possible. You can probably tell by my baritone voice that I'm hoping to start a singing career. These other guys need to get out too. They may not have a great career path like me, but they're my friends, and really good guys."

The calf, unlike the others, had no white spots on his back, sides or belly. He was solid black, but had a white, star-shaped spot between his eyes, which reminded Cata of some horses she'd seen. He had stuck his snout through the bars of his pen to talk to her, and then he lowered it to sip from the water trough below. He looked at Cata when she came to sit near his pen and sniffed in her direction.

"That's what I'm here for, cow. I'm trying to get information on the people who work here. Once we know what they're doing to you animals, I can alert the authorities."

"I am not a cow, nor are the others in these pens. Cows are girls and we are young males. You may refer to us as steers if you like."

"I do apologize. I'm a city cat so I don't know much about farm animals. What about the research that goes on here? Do you know anything that might help me?"

34

"The people here are all right for the most part, but there are a couple who've been really mean to us. One is the head guy, Ackerman, and the other is also a man. He's almost always with Ackerman and I don't trust him. I think his name is Darrell. They always tell me to shut up and stop mooing. Sometimes Ackerman hits me too. I don't dare sing around them, even though I swear it's in my blood, because I'm afraid of what they might do to me. I heard them talking the other day and Ackerman said, "When we start the experiments, let's do that noisy calf first. I'm sick of his mooing". I have a feeling they're going to do something horrible to us and I'm really scared, so I'll help you anyway I can. I may not be able to hold onto things, but I can ram somebody with my head if you need me to."

"What's your name, steer?"

"Caruso, at least that's what the farmer used to call me before I ended up here. Some men came to our farm one night and stole us. As you can imagine, we were pretty surprised to end up here."

"That's terrible. Your owner must really miss you and your songs. What else can you tell me about this Ackerman before I leave?"

"He keeps watching me and I think he suspects that I can both talk and sing. I've tried to cut down on my singing, but it's hard to do because I have to express what I feel in my heart."

"You must be very careful from now on, Caruso. We believe that Ackerman is a dangerous man. If he finds out that you can talk, let alone sing, who knows what could happen? Be smart about your singing for just a little while longer. Maybe there will be a way we can get you and your friends back home again," Cata said.

"That would be wonderful. We really miss our farmer. He talked to us and fed us sweet hay, not the awful stuff they give us here. It's like birdseed."

"I'd like to stay and chat with you longer, but I need to get going and check in with my supervisor soon. Before I do though, I need to find out where the scientists work. Do you know where I can find them?"

"It's lunch time, so most of them will be in the room down the hall. It has a sign on the door that I can't read, but there's a big red light over the door, so you can't miss it."

"Thanks, Caruso, I passed that room on my way to find you. I'll get to work right away and find out as much as I can about these people and their experiments. I'll come back to see you as soon as I can, and I promise I won't forget about any of you."

"Thank you, cat."

"That's Cata, Cata Hari."

Cata left as quietly as she had arrived, like most cats do, and carried on to the room with the sign and the red light. The door was slightly ajar and she saw people sitting and chatting. Some wore white coats, and others were dressed in coveralls. They were all so preoccupied with their conversations about television shows and sports that it was easy for her to slip into the room unnoticed. She found a dark corner and settled in, hoping to hear valuable information that she could pass along to Max.

Anyone who looked at Cata would think that she was just another pretty cat, but inside she was very upset. In fact, she had gotten angrier with each group of animals she had seen because of how they'd been treated. But she knew it was important to keep those feelings to herself and try her best to forget her anger because she needed to pay very close attention to what the people in the room said. She had heard the stories of the animals in cages, but now it was time to hear what the workers had to say. She could only hope that their conversations would be more interesting than just more talk about sports and television. She knew what Max expected of her and didn't want to let him down, nor did she want to let down the animals.

CHAPTER 9

Mustafa Senses Danger

Like Cata, Mustafa learned to talk when he was young, and his vocabulary was expanded with the help of his mother. In fact, Mustafa had such an impressive command of the English language that Cata often told him that had he been born a human, he would probably have made and excellent university professor. However, the dog had also been born with another gift that needed no teaching. He had the ability to sense danger when others could not, including other dogs. He always told Cata when she left on a mission that he would know she was in trouble when he heard the swish of her tail, but it was merely a joke between friends.

Other dogs could certainly tell when a wild animal was in the yard at night through their acute senses of smell and hearing. Mustafa could certainly do that too, but he was different from other dogs. He simply had a way of knowing when something was going to happen, whether he was awake or sleeping, and he was never wrong. He always knew when Cata was in trouble, and for her, just knowing that Mustafa would always come when she needed extra help on a mission gave her a sense of fearlessness.

But for now, Mustafa slept on the floor, halfway between the front door and the foot of the stairs to the upper storey of the house. It was his spot, a position in the house where he felt he would be most effective if something happened in the night, just in case he had to lead his pack out the door or hurry up the steps to rescue them. He was dreaming about running through the forest and how wonderful it was to feel the leaves and branches brushing against his thick fur. His legs were moving while he slept and dreamt, but then they slowed to a stop as his dream changed.

Now he was in a large, white room filled with all types of animals who seemed to be frightened. He wandered from one end of the room to the other looking at rabbits, calves, monkeys, pigs, and dogs, all beagles, his favorite. His inner danger warning system began to grow and it woke him up with a start. He stood up, shook his thick coat and they laid back down again. It was not an emergency because the warning system was still at low, but he knew it had to have something to do with Cata's mission.

This had never happened so early into one of Cata's missions and he wasn't sure if he should be worried or not. He mulled the situation over in his mind and decided to speak with Cata as soon as she returned home. She could be facing many dangerous situations in her mission at the research centre and he wondered if it would be better all around if Max Wolf's human agents took over from Cata.

Instead of going back to sleep, he got up and walked to the bay window in the living room and looked out at the gray sky. He sat for a while watching a squirrel try to get seeds and nuts from the bird feeder. He wasn't fond of squirrels at all, and with nothing else outside to entertain him, he returned to his spot and settled slowly back into sleep. While Mustafa dreamt, Cata was about to make her first important discovery, and it was one she hoped to never make again.

CHAPTER 10

Doctor Linus Ackerman

The smell of food was making Cata hungry while she listened to the discussion the staff of the animal centre had over lunch. So far, she hadn't heard anything of value to her investigation, just a lot of talk about hockey and reality TV. Neither interested her because when she had time off, she mainly slept or discussed world events with Mustafa. Just when she thought it was time to leave to meet with Max, a man in a white coat entered the room. The workers stopped what they were doing to give him their full attention, and Cata was convinced one or two of them looked scared.

The man in the white coat looked around the room as if he were counting heads. He was tall and slender, and Cata thought he might be quite handsome if he wasn't sneering. She instinctively disliked him and suspected he might be Dr. Ackerman, or perhaps he was his assistant, Darrell. He began barking orders at the workers and Cata almost jumped at the loudness of his voice. She lowered her head and tried to make herself as small as possible because she knew she could become part of an experiment herself if she was discovered. It sounded as if something big was going to happen, and Cata listened carefully while remaining on guard.

"Where is the cat?" the scientist asked.

The workers looked at each other and shook their heads. Only Casper looked at no one, and instead he concentrated on his lunch. Ackerman singled him out, directing the same question at him.

"I don't know anything about a cat, Dr. Ackerman. Are you doing experiments on them now?" Casper asked.

"Don't be stupid. You know we don't experiment on cats. I was reviewing the security tapes and there was a cat in this building yesterday. Its mainly grey with a little white and beige, you can't miss it. We can't afford to have a stray animal wandering about the place and messing up our experiments. All of you keep an eye out for this cat, and when you find it, bring it to me."

"When do the calf experiments start, Dr. Ackerman?" asked the technician Cata had seen earlier in the rabbit room.

"We'll be doing those experiments this week and will hopefully finish by Friday, but nothing happens until I have my hands on that cat. Now all of you, get back to work."

Dr. Ackerman turned on his heel and exited the room. Cata saw a small, younger man follow him out and assumed he must be Darrell. Cata was quite frightened and knew she had to get out of the building as soon as possible. Now she'd have to be even more careful since all the workers would be looking for her. On the positive side though, until

Ackerman found her, he wouldn't hurt Caruso or the other calves. From her hiding place, she looked around the room at the faces of the workers. The only one she was sure she could trust was Casper.

Casper didn't know what to do after Ackerman left. The problem was that he knew exactly where the cat was because it had been under his chair the whole time Ackerman shouted his orders to them. He knew the cat was in the building because he had seen her earlier in the rabbit room. He pretended he hadn't because he had the feeling she didn't want to be seen. There was no chance he would ever tell Ackerman though, because he had a feeling that the scientist had something nasty in mind for the poor cat.

Casper stared at the rest of his sandwich and realized he'd lost his appetite. He got ready to leave, but when no one was looking he broke the remainder of his sandwich into small pieces and set them on the floor. He thought that, at the very least, he could keep her presence a secret and give her something to fill her tummy too. He bent down to look at the cat under his chair and winked at her. He was most surprised when the cat winked back.

***

What Casper didn't know, and couldn't possibly even guess, was that Ackerman already knew something very important about Cata Hari. He had seen her move her mouth in an odd way when he reviewed the research centre security tapes from the previous day, and he suspected she was a rare animal who could speak. It was the second time he'd come across this, at least he thought it was. Late one evening when he'd been checking on the calves, he'd looked through the observation window before entering the room where they were housed. First, he saw one of the calves move his lips strangely. Then he heard Italian opera singing, but when he opened the door to investigate, the calf quickly lowered his head to drink from the water trough. At first, Ackerman thought he was losing his mind. But now, with the tape of the cat, he was convinced that some animals could speak. He needed to take apart the voice boxes of the cat and calf to discover the secret of their speech. That would not only make him famous but make him a very rich man too.

Linus Ackerman had been a well-respected scientist. Indeed, he was a smart man who had directed research at a university laboratory for several years. Then one day his experiments stopped working and he found he'd come up against a brick wall. Eventually the money for his work ran out, and he couldn't get more because he had run out of good ideas.

He was embarrassed when he was fired, but he was without a job for only a few weeks. The animal research centre hired him for the position of director because they were so impressed with their ability to attract a well-known scientist away from the university. What they didn't know, because he had lied to them in his interview, was that he had been fired from his previous job.

Ackerman wanted to show the world he was still a brilliant scientist, but he also wanted to get back at the cows and steers of the world. When he was a boy, he used to cut through a farmer's field on his way to school, until the day he was chased by a steer and almost stabbed by its horns. He had lost his knapsack while running and he was yelled at by his teacher in front of the whole class for not having his homework assignment. Not only that, but he got a week of detentions too. After that, he had hated anything to do with cows and steers, even though he should not have trespassed on the farmer's field in the first place.

He couldn't wait to experiment on Caruso and the other calves. No one outside the research centre knew about the calves because he had bought them illegally. He wanted animals to do secret experiments on and he had hired someone to steal the calves. But once he discovered that the one calf could sing, he cancelled those experiments. Now he was even happier he'd bought the calves because if he hadn't, he would

44

never have discovered the singing steer. That discovery would be sure to make him famous, and he marveled about how clever he was. He was convinced that it wouldn't be long before people started admiring his work again, and then he thought out loud saying, "I am smarter than most people, and once I've found the secret of talking animals, everyone will know that. Plus, I'll be a very rich man!"

CHAPTER 11

Mustafa to the Rescue

Ackerman took everything out on the employees of the animal research group whether it was because he was in a bad mood, or because he was downright mean. The employees were mainly students who worked at the research centre for one term in order to gain experience with animals. All the students in the biology department at the university had to take the course, and they were afraid to speak up when Ackerman acted badly towards them or the animals in case he gave them a bad grade. However, the latest group of students were more vocal, and two of them hoped to find enough evidence against Ackerman to report him to the university.

Julia Lemming and Gerald Otterman had met several times to discuss Ackerman, his assistant Darrell, and the tests they were doing on the animals. Both were sure some of the testing was not legal, and they felt it was just a matter of time before they had enough proof to expose Ackerman. Looking for proof against Ackerman was dangerous for them to begin with, and now they had a cat to be concerned about too. Neither of them had seen it yet, but both were keeping an eye out in hopes that they could protect the poor animal. They knew their only possible friend in helping the cat and the other animals was Casper, the janitor. He was the one who always spoke up for the animals, and they both suspected that he had complained to the authorities about Ackerman in the past.

***

Cata was still in the lunchroom and keeping as quiet as possible as she thought about how to leave without being seen, especially now that everyone would be looking for her. She had nibbled on part of the sandwich, and could have eaten more, because it was salmon salad, one of her favorites, but she saw an opportunity to slip out of the room. Casper had stood up and was talking to the others in the room and Cata was certain he had done it so that she could escape without notice. She headed straight to the room where Caruso lived, but didn't enter because she heard the voice of Ackerman inside yelling at the poor calf. She couldn't make out what the scientist was saying, but it sounded scary. If Emma talked to her that way, she would probably hide under the bed.

Cata knew she had to stop Ackerman before he could carry out his experiment on Caruso, but first she needed to meet with Max. She had to report to him that Ackerman had seen her in the research centre, and Max also needed to know about the danger to Caruso. After that, she wanted to get home because she was tired and hungry. She was also eager to speak with Mustafa because she believed she would need his help to defeat Ackerman.

47

Cata waited in the loading dock, making sure she was well hidden from the security camera, until she heard a delivery truck pull up outside the building. When the door to the loading dock began to lift and she felt it was safe, she ran out and down the steps. Had she looked behind her, she would have seen a man in a white lab coat. The man was running fast because he knew that Ackerman would reward him if he was able to catch the cat, but before he could get close enough to her, she jumped through the open window of Max Wolf's waiting car. The man ran to his own car to follow them because he needed to know where the cat lived. Cata did not know she was being chased, nor did Max realize the man was running after Cata Hari. Max sped away from the curb as soon as Cata settled in the seat beside him. They didn't know that danger was upon them, or that the chase was not yet over.

**

Although they were not aware of being followed, Max had been a spy for years and he always drove with caution, out of habit. He took several turns on the way to Cata's house. Anyone watching would think he was lost, but he knew what he was doing and drove down streets only to double back the opposite way and then take an unexpected shortcut through a parking lot to yet another street. The man following in his car lost sight of them when Max pulled into an alley. There, Max and Cata talked about the mission and what she had discovered while he removed the camera from her collar. Max was most concerned that Cata had not only been seen by Ackerman, but the man wanted her found.

"Cata, I'm worried about your safety. I need to go over the pictures you've taken, understand the layout of the facility, and report to my own supervisor. I want you to take tomorrow off and get some rest. We'll meet at our usual spot the day after tomorrow."

"You know best, Max, and I don't mind getting some extra sleep."

"Next time, I'll fit you with a special camera, one that will live-stream directly to my computer. You'll be able to film Ackerman and the workers, and I'll be able to hear their conversation too. Even better, I'll be able to back you up if there's any trouble."

"Okay Max, and I'll let Mustafa know what's going on. He may be able to help too."

Max pulled out of the alley and drove in the direction of Cata's home, unaware that their pursuer had found them again. He parked a few doors away from the house and watched as Cata trotted elegantly down the street. He didn't drive off until she was safely through the cat door. Normally he didn't worry about Cata this much when she was working for him, but he had a funny feeling that danger lay ahead. He knew she had some sort of guardian, although he'd never seen him in action. He didn't know who it was because Cata was secretive about him. He only knew that his name was Mustafa.

Max tried to shrug off the feeling of danger he felt. After all, with the information from the pictures on Cata's camera on his side, and the verbal report Cata had provided, the authorities, including the local police, would have no choice but give their approval for the next part of the mission. Once he had proof of Ackerman's crimes, or at the first sign of danger for Cata, he would call on his own agents and the police for help. He had a feeling that he might also meet Mustafa this time.

After Max drove away, a man stopped to stare at Cata's house. There was nothing about his appearance that would attract the attention of passersby, he was just an ordinary man with a shopping bag. He then hurried down the street, turned the corner to the next street, crossed through a yard, and climbed over a fence to enter the back garden of Cata's house. He ran to the back of the house, mounted the steps, and turned the handle of the door. He sighed with relief when he found it was unlocked. "This will be so easy. I can grab the cat and be gone in seconds."

He entered the kitchen, set down the shopping bag, and knelt down to remove a pet carrier cage from the bag. He was ready to look for the cat, put her in the cage, and run back to his car. However, when he looked up, he found himself nose to nose with a large German shepherd who growled and bared his teeth in welcome. The man scrambled to his feet, but when the dog put both front paws on his shoulders, he screamed, dropped the cage, and fled through the door to the backyard. He ran as fast as he could, but the shepherd was gaining on him and snapping at his heels. He threw himself headlong over the fence and didn't feel safe until he had made it around the corner to his car. He had already told Ackerman that the cat would be delivered that day, and now he would have to report his failed attempt, and one thing Ackerman did not like was failure.

Mustafa barked until the man was out of sight and then, satisfied that he would not return, ran back inside the house. He pushed his rump against the inside of the door to close it and saw Cata pacing near the stove.

"Mustafa, I think that man was from the research building, the place I've been checking out for Max. Do you think he was trying to catnap me?"

"I do indeed, Cata. That cage is the ideal size for a cat. He made a big mistake by coming here though, and if he comes back, I'll do more than just chase him. I'll never let him hurt you, but I think you need to get in touch with Max. After all, what if Emma had been home and he tried to take her too?"

"You're right, this could have been much worse, and Max could certainly help with more protection, but I won't see him for a couple of days, Mustafa. He had to leave town to meet with his boss, so we'll have to be on our toes until then, just in case that man comes back."

"I think we've seen the last of him, Cata. If he does come back, he'd better bring someone to help him, because I have no plans of letting my guard down. You had better keep close to Emma tonight, just in case. I'll split my sleeping time between the front and back doors."

"Mustafa, what about the cage?"

"Let the humans find it. I have a feeling they'll call the police once they notice it, especially when they see that the back door is unlocked and the flowerpots on the porch have been knocked over. If they don't notice at first, we can act really upset and needy to get their attention."

"I sometimes wonder how they'd survive without us," Cata said.

CHAPTER 12

Evidence of a Break-in

Emma's parents were both successful and enjoyed their jobs. Her father, George Barrett, was a professor at the university where he was considered an expert on climate change. Her mother, Candace, was an architect who was currently designing the building for the new main library. Perhaps it came to Emma naturally, or perhaps it was because her parents always encouraged her to learn about new things, but she was a very bright student. She was usually ahead at least two chapters in all her subjects, and because of that, her teacher let her work in the school library one afternoon almost every week. She loved reading books and enjoyed working there so much that the time always flew by quickly. That afternoon, the time had indeed gotten away from her, and it was the librarian who reminded her that classes had been over for quite some time and it was time for her to leave the school to go home.

When Emma didn't arrive home from school at her usual time, Mustafa began to worry that the man who broke into the house may have wanted to kidnap her instead of Cata, but then he remembered that the cage left behind in the kitchen wasn't big enough for the girl to fit inside. He hoped she would arrive soon because he wanted her safe at home so that he could protect her. He also needed a walk badly and had given up pacing the floor of the hallway to sit at the living room bay window. From there he could see down the street and watch for her. Eventually Mustafa saw her running along the sidewalk toward the house and he went to the front door to wait for her with his leash in his mouth.

"Poor Mustafa, I'm so sorry to be late. You must be ready to burst by now. Let's go to the park and we'll take our time so you can have a good run too."

Cata hoped that Mustafa would have shown Emma the evidence in the kitchen as soon as she got home, but the cat also understood her friend's need to go to the bathroom. After all, he didn't use a litter box like her. Cata had never been one to waste time doing nothing, so she sat by the front door and cleaned her paws with her tongue while she waited for them to return home after Mustafa's well needed run in the park. She also thought Mustafa had earned an extra long walk after the braveness he'd shown that afternoon.

She thought about her mission and decided it would be best to stay home the following day, especially since the cat-napper might wait in hiding for her somewhere outside the house. She was tired from her work at the research centre anyway and thought a day of sleep could only help her be as alert as possible for the next part of the mission. She stood when she heard the key in the lock and began to run toward the kitchen but stopped halfway there. If she waited where she was, she could lure Emma to the room and that way the little girl would see the cage and the evidence of the break-in.

When they returned from their walk, Cata waited while Emma removed Mustafa's leash, then she started for the kitchen so that the girl would follow.

"Smokey, you must be hungry too. I think both you and Mustafa should have a treat, and I'll join you with a cookie and a glass of milk," Emma said.

She followed her pets into the kitchen and got treats for them both, but when she sat at the kitchen table to eat her cookies and milk, she saw the cage on the floor.

"Hmm, I didn't see that this morning. I wonder if we're going on a trip." She looked at the animals and said, "Maybe you're coming with us!"

She got up to inspect the cage and then noticed the dirt and grass on the kitchen floor. She went to unlock the kitchen door but found to her surprise that it wasn't even locked. When she looked through the screen door, she saw the fallen flowerpots and spilled soil all over the back porch and shook her head. She knew her mother loved her planters so she decided to go outside and clean up the mess. Mustafa had other ideas though. He took the girl's wrist in his mouth gently and pulled her back inside the house. Then he barked several times to make sure she paid attention to him.

"What are you doing, Mustafa? What's up with you today? All I want to do is try to clean up for Mom and Dad. Mom will be awfully upset that one of the planters is broken."

She went out the door again and Mustafa followed barking and jumping until she stopped. Then he herded the little girl toward the door, like a lost sheep, pushing and barking until she went back inside the kitchen. Emma didn't understand what he was doing and stooped down to gaze into the dog's eyes.

"I sure wish you could talk, Mustafa, because you're acting like you know something, like there's something really wrong."

Mustafa glanced away from the girl to look at Cata, but the cat moved her head slightly from side to side, warning the dog not to speak to the girl. They would have no end of trouble in their lives if the humans ever found out they could talk. Just then the front door slammed, and recognizing the voices of George and Candace, the dog and cat started on their extreme attention-getting behaviors. Mustafa, a normally quiet dog, began barking up a storm, while Cata ran into the hall where she meowed and hissed, and then ran back to the kitchen.

"Mom, Dad, there's something funny going on," Emma yelled from the kitchen.

George and Candace were alarmed at the behavior of the animals and ran to the kitchen to make sure Emma was all right. Mustafa rose on his back legs and planted his front paws squarely on George's shoulders. He had no intention of stopping his unusual behaviour until his owners paid attention to the cage on the floor of the kitchen and the mess on the porch.

George Barrett was a solidly built man and easily accepted Mustafa's weight. He worked out regularly at the gym, and almost every weekend he and Candace ran a few kilometers. They wanted to keep in shape, but also had hopes of entering long distance races to raise money for charity. Both George and Candace were fit enough to have handled the intruder had they been home, but they were lucky to have a smart dog like Mustafa to take care of things in their absence. George knew Mustafa was trying to warn him and encouraged him back down to the floor.

"Good boy, Mustafa. You're telling us that something happened here today, aren't you?" Mustafa moved to face the kitchen door and whined. When George tried to unlock it, he found it wasn't necessary. "Emma, did you unlock the door when you came home?"

"No Dad, it was like that when I got home, and the flowerpots are knocked over, and Mustafa wouldn't let me clean them up. He actually pushed me back inside the house and he was barking like crazy," Emma said.

"Good boy, Mustafa," George said again as he stroked the dog's back.

"Do you think we had a break in?" Candace asked.

George looked out the door, and then opened the outside screen door, but before he could venture out, Mustafa ran past him toward the back of the garden. He turned back to make sure his owners were following, and then he lowered his head to the ground to sniff at footprints in the soil. The intruder had made the prints when he arrived and also when he launched himself over the fence. The man was terrified of what the dog would do to him and in his haste to get over the fence, he had crushed several flowers underfoot. George looked carefully at the ground and could see that there were two sets of footprints, one pointing toward the house and a second pointing away. He was convinced that someone had indeed broken into the house and his fearless German shepherd had chased the intruder off.

"Maybe I left the back door unlocked by mistake. I usually check that it's locked before bed, but I guess I must have forgotten to do so last night," George said.

"Whoever it was left something in the kitchen, Dad. It's a cage, like the type you put a cat in when you're traveling. I think they were trying to steal Smokey."

When Smokey heard her name, she looked at the humans and ran back to the house. She waited for them to open the door and then ran upstairs to hide in Emma's room. She had a feeling it would take a while for the humans to sort everything out, which meant dinner would likely be late. In the meantime, she could start catching up on her sleep with a catnap.

CHAPTER 13

Protecting Cata

The police asked many questions of George and Candace Barrett and the couple had no trouble providing answers. When it came to their cat Smokey however, they had no explanation as to why a cat-napper would have tried to steal her. When Cata woke from her nap and came down the stairs, looking for dinner, the police officer saw her and commented on what a beautiful animal she was. Candace was distressed that something might happen to Smokey and knew her daughter would be heart-broken if it did, so she asked the officer if they could provide protection while she and George were away from the house. Crime had been low across the city and the officer's request for a watch on the house was agreed to by his supervisor, at least for a few days. George and Candace wondered about having a security system installed and the officer explained that it certainly wouldn't hurt. Mustafa snorted and left the room when he heard the comment because he felt insulted. He knew he was a better security system than any mechanical contraption.

Upstairs, Emma was busy preparing for another test the following day. It was hard for her to concentrate because she was worried about her cat. She kept at it though and found she was well-prepared within an hour. There would be more time for review before bed. When she went downstairs for dinner, she was pleased to see that her parents had ordered food from their favorite Chinese restaurant. While she played with her spring roll, she begged her parents to let her stay home from school the next day so that she could take care of Smokey, but they wouldn't hear of it.

"Sweetheart, we know you're mature for your age, and responsible too, but it could be dangerous for you to stay at home. Plus, you have a test tomorrow," Candace said.

When Emma left for school the following morning, she gave Smokey and Mustafa extra hugs. The police had just arrived to set up watch on the house from an unmarked car on the street, and the officer parked a few spaces down from the house, so as not to attract a burglar's attention. He was clearly very good at his job since Emma would never have thought the man in the car was a policeman. Between the police and Mustafa, she knew she shouldn't be concerned about Smokey's safety. She couldn't help but worry though and knew she would have to try her best to be patient during classes that day until she could get home to make sure her cat was safe.

***

Max had visited headquarters to meet with his superiors, and they were not only pleased with the progress of the mission but had given their approval for the second stage. He decided to return home a day early, and although he had no meeting with Cata until the following day, he still had a feeling that there was danger. To satisfy his nagging worry, he drove past Cata's house and immediately spotted the unmarked police car parked on the street. He walked to the car and showed his credentials to the officer who described the events of the previous day at the Barrett house and Max knew he'd had good reason to be worried about danger. He was alarmed but knew he couldn't even attempt to see Cata until their regular appointment. If he made a fuss at this point, the mission, and Cata, could be put at risk. Cata wasn't just a secret agent for him, he was also quite fond of her and knew he would have to be extra careful to keep her safe.

He returned to his car and drove to his office. He still had some time to work before leaving for dinner and used it to examine every detail of the final part of Cata's mission, looking for any hint of a problem. He had the camera ready, the one that would stream to his laptop in real time. He had also selected several agents under his command to be ready to help Cata, should she need it. But he was still worried, so just to be on the safe side, he went over the whole mission plan again to make sure that all his bases were covered. He was that concerned about Cata's safety.

***

"What do you mean you failed? You said it wouldn't be a problem. I want that cat, and I want it as soon as possible. Go back to the house tomorrow, and this time don't be such a sniveling coward. You work with dogs all the time, so you should be able to manage one measly German shepherd. Better yet just go and order another cage and I'll find someone else to do the job. Honestly, if I don't do it myself, it doesn't get done!"

Darrell Krump, the would-be "cat" burglar, returned to his desk and picked up the telephone receiver. He ordered another animal carrier cage from the supply room and then returned to his regular work, angry that he had let his boss down. He was as disappointed with himself as his boss was, but how was he to know that a German shepherd would be inside the house? He didn't think it was fair that he was expected to steal a cat when a big dog like that was growling at him and threatening to attack him, even if it was his idea to break into the house in the first place.

Darrell wasn't particularly fond of Linus Ackerman, but he wanted to gain a higher position within the research centre and eventually take over when the man retired. Like many of the others at the research building, he was a graduate student getting experience working with animals. However, his grades in the other courses he had taken were not good at all, plus he was getting nowhere with his own research project. He knew that he would soon be expelled from the university and wanted to make sure he got a permanent job with Ackerman before that happened. Now he would have to find another way to suck up to Ackerman and get into his good books once more.

He saw Gerald Otterman sitting and talking quietly with Julia Lemming. He had noticed that they seemed to spend quite a lot of time together during working hours and wondered what they found so interesting. He didn't trust either one of them. In fact, he was certain that they were plotting against him. One of Darrell's problems was that he thought almost everyone was plotting against him.

Gerald and Julia noticed Darrell watching them and they both returned to their work. Julia sneaked looks at Darrell while she tidied her desk. She had never liked him, not from the beginning, and now that Gerald had told her that he saw Darrell running from the building yesterday before their shift was over, she was suspicious. She knew that if she or Gerald had left early like that, Ackerman would have reported them to the university.

She continued to look at Darrell, cautiously, when he wasn't looking. He seemed upset and unable to concentrate on the tasks in front of him. She wondered about the other thing Gerald had mentioned. He had overheard Ackerman yelling at Darrell, something about a cat and a German shepherd. They assumed it was the cat they'd heard about the day before, but the German shepherd was something new. They didn't use such big dogs in their research, and neither she nor Gerald could figure out what it was all about. They would observe closely to see what happened over the next few days, and certainly keep their eyes open for the cat so they could protect it. One thing that made both students happy though was that Darrell, who was Ackerman's golden boy, had disappointed the boss and hopefully he wouldn't be as smug as he had been in the past.

CHAPTER 14

Mustafa to the Rescue Again

Cata had woken early to say goodbye to Emma before she left for school, and then she'd curled up again beside the girl's pillow to go back to sleep. At just past noon she stretched and lay on her back with her limbs dangling to each side. She was dozing again when Mustafa entered the room.

"Hey, Cata, it's time to get up, unless you plan to sleep forever. What's on your schedule for today?"

"I'm awake, Mustafa, I was just resting my eyes. First, I'm going to have something to eat because I am quite hungry this morning. Then I will clean my paws and face and leave to go to the fish and seafood store, just in case Max shows up. I was going to stay home today,

Mustafa, but having thought about it overnight, I think I might actually be safer outside than inside."

"I don't know, Cata. What if the catnapper is watching the house and he sees you leave? He could nab you and be away in seconds, especially if he has a car. If he works fast, the policeman in the car down the street might miss the whole thing."

"Don't worry, Mustafa, Max taught me long ago how to lose a tail if I'm being followed. I promise I won't be gone long. I'll just see Max and then come straight home."

"Lose a tail, eh? That's funny. But listen, Cata, the policeman will see you when you go through the cat door and he'll put you back in the house."

"Emma forgot to close her window. I can sneak out that way, it's only one floor down."

"You're very stubborn, Cata, and one of these days your luck will run out you know," Mustafa called out as Cata ran down the stairs. She knew she was taking a chance, but she had a gut feeling that it was important to leave the house. She went to her food bowl to eat while Mustafa continued to lecture her. After she cleaned herself, she wished the dog a good afternoon and ran back up the stairs to Emma's room. She balanced on the outer windowsill for a few moments and leapt to the ground, landing on her feet, as cats always do.

***

Max Wolf didn't sleep very well and the next day he had a nagging feeling that Cata Hari needed him. He decided to go to the fish and seafood store, just in case the cat was waiting for him. He grabbed his coat and hat, said goodbye to assistant, Sally Swan, and headed out of the building to his car. Minutes later he parked in the downtown and walked to the fish store. From a distance, he could not see Cata Hari, but as he got closer, he saw a tail disappear around the side of the store, like a wisp of smoke. He followed and found Cata behind the store, pacing back and forth with her tail twitching. Stooping down, he stroked the cat's head and the length of her back, finishing by scratching the side of her face, as she liked best.

"I had a feeling you wanted to see me today. I spoke to the policeman on your street and he told me what happened yesterday. Are you all right, Cata?"

"Oh yes, Mustafa was very brave and chased the man away. I think it was someone from the research centre. Do you think they've figured out that I can talk?"

"I suppose it's possible that someone overheard you, but it's probably more likely that they saw your mouth move when they reviewed their security tapes. We'll never know for certain until we can talk to someone inside the research centre. That won't happen until you crack the case though, Cata. Are you still willing to start the final part of the mission?"

"Absolutely, Max. I think they're going to do something to Caruso the calf soon. Dr. Ackerman doesn't like him very much, and I don't understand why because he seems quite lovely to me. When do we start on the next part of the mission?"

"Let's stick to the original plan and you can go in tomorrow," he said. He winked at Cata Hari and she did the same back.

Max knew that if Ackerman had tried to kidnap Cata, then it was possible that he had someone from the research centre watching them as they spoke, maybe even someone who could read lips. He continued to describe a fake plan to her. The real plan would happen that night, not the next day, and the details would be revealed to her when he was positive that they were alone and away from prying eyes. When Max finished, Cata wound herself around his legs, meowed, and then looked at him with pleading eyes. Max put his hand over his mouth and whispered to her.

"Okay Cata, you go to our secret place and be very careful that you're not followed. I'll get an order of fish and chips and meet you in a few minutes. We can talk about the real plan there."

Cata was pleased that she had managed to wheedle an extra meal out of her boss, and she headed for the park. She used the tools that Max had taught her, taking a route that would make it almost impossible for anyone to follow her. It was far easier for a cat than a human to lose someone following them because they could fit in smaller places. When she got to the park, she dove for shelter from watching eyes under their usual picnic table and waited for Max to arrive. She didn't care much for chips, but her mouth was already watering with the thought of eating a nice piece of fish.

***

Mustafa sat in his spot in the hall and patiently watched the cat door. He had sensed danger all afternoon and hoped Cata would come home soon so that he could protect her. He was about to move to the bay window in the living room to check outside when his ears perked up. There was a noise coming from the direction of the kitchen, and he got up to investigate.

There was no one in the kitchen when he arrived, but he heard the doorknob rattle. He chose not to bark, deciding instead to remain quiet and surprise the intruder when the door opened. Then I'll really teach him a lesson, he thought. It was his home after all, and he would protect it against the type of person who would sink so low as to steal a little girl's cat. The noises continued as someone fiddled with the lock on the door. Mustafa was hidden from anyone entering by a curve in the kitchen counter and would have the advantage of being able to see the intruder first.

When the door opened, Mustafa waited behind the kitchen counter, and then at just the right time he launched himself at the intruder. He bit the man's arm and barked into his face. When the man tried to break free from the dog, Mustafa lunged down and got a firm hold on the man's ankle. The Barrett's neighbour, Annie Finch, was weeding in her flower garden and looked up when she heard the commotion from the Barrett's house. When she leaned across the fence and saw Mustafa struggling with a stranger in the kitchen, she ran from her yard to the street and alerted the police officer keeping watch from the car a few houses down.

Being a good dog, Mustafa released his hold on the man's ankle when the police officer arrived. He sat proudly but continued his low, throaty growl while the officer handcuffed the intruder. He was a large man dressed in black and wearing a hat, also black, that was pulled down low on his brow. One thing Mustafa knew for certain was that he was not the same man who visited the house the day before. This man looked fierce and was much bigger. He also didn't look like what Mustafa thought a scientist should, and he just knew that the man was a criminal. He shuddered inside when he thought of what such a monster could do to poor Cata. Mustafa knew the second break-in could not be a simple coincidence and concluded that the research centre probably hired a real criminal to kidnap Cata rather than send one of their own people. He barked his approval when the officer led the man out of the house and put him in the back seat of his car.

After the police officer drove away, Mustafa paced in the hallway. He didn't know where Cata was, whether she'd returned through the upstairs window, or if the man might have taken her. He could have done that first, shoved her in his car, and then decided to rob the house afterward. He ran up the stairs to Emma's room and inched the door open with his snout. Mustafa breathed a sigh of relief because Cata had indeed climbed up the trellis outside and entered Emma's bedroom. She was sound asleep on the bed and he backed quietly out of the room, so as not to disturb her. Mustafa returned to his place at the bottom of the stairs because the excitement was over and it was as good a time as any to catch up on his own sleep. Mustafa slept peacefully and neither he nor Cata woke until Emma and her parents came home. George and Candace had left work early and picked their daughter up from school after hearing from the police about the second break-in, the man's capture, and how brave Mustafa was.

CHAPTER 15

Cata's Investigation Heats Up

"You've been eating fish, Cata, I can smell it from here. Does Max convince you to go on these crazy missions through your stomach? I think you should tell him to get someone else to do the next part of your mission, because there could be even more dangerous people at that research centre than the man who broke into our house today. You could be playing with fire."

"I've already said yes to Max, Mustafa, and I can't possibly go back on my word now. Besides, they caught the cat-napper this afternoon, and I don't think anyone at the research centre is dangerous, except for Ackerman. Don't worry, Mustafa. I'll be careful tonight and I always have you to help if I do get into trouble."

"But Cata, be reasonable. If they hired that thug to take you from here, they could have hired another one to try to hurt you or put you in a cage at that awful research centre. Remember, you're a cat, not a superhero."

"Stop being such a worrier, Mustafa. I'll be fine."

"You are annoyingly stubborn, Cata, but I'll stay awake tonight in case you need help. Just promise me you really will be careful. Don't take any foolish chances and don't hang around there any longer than you need to."

Cata rubbed her jaw against Mustafa's front leg and then repeated it with the other side of her face. She loved Mustafa and hated to worry him, but she was an undercover agent with a job to do. After promising to be as careful as possible, she trotted softly to the cat door and slipped through into the cool of the night. Even though Ackerman said the calf experiments wouldn't begin until she was caught, she had a feeling there would indeed be one that night, one involving Caruso, and she needed to save him.

***

Cata met Max at their picnic table in the park for the second time in one day. He fitted her with the new camera and drove her to the research centre, timing it with a rare evening delivery of scientific supplies. As usual, Cata had no trouble getting into the building through the loading dock door. She ran toward the hallway where Caruso and the other steers lived and had almost reached her hiding place behind the mop and bucket when she bumped into Casper.

"What are you doing back here? You shouldn't be here at any time, not when Ackerman is looking for you, and especially not tonight. He's doing his big experiment, and you could end up on the wrong side of a scalpel if you're not careful."

Casper had a fondness for all animals, but he loved cats and bent down to pet her. He loved the beautiful grays in her coat, some betraying just a hint of beige. He was about to say something more to the cat when he heard the voice of the one person he despised more than anyone else in the world.

"What are you doing, Casper Fox? I pay you to work, not dally in the hallways."

It was Linus Ackerman, and fortunately for Cata, he hadn't seen her because she was hidden from view by Casper's body. To divert the scientist's attention, Casper got down on his hands and knees, pulled a rag from his back pocket and pretended to clean the floor.

"Dr. Ackerman, I found some water on the floor here and I'm making sure it's dry, so no one slips and takes a fall. I'll be getting to my other chores next."

"Make sure you get all of it done as soon as possible. We have big things happening tonight and it's important to stay on schedule. I need you to help the workers move that noisy calf into the operating room, no later than midnight."

"Yes sir, Dr. Ackerman," Casper said.

Once Ackerman had left, Casper picked Cata up and looked at her lovingly. If he couldn't protect the calf, then at least he could give the cat some advice to keep her safe.

"Just between you and me, I'd like to punch that Ackerman's lights out, but that's beside the point right now. You can't stay here, it's just too dangerous. Ackerman has warned everyone to be on the look out for you. You could end up in a cage, or he might do an experiment on you too."

Cata gazed into Casper's blue eyes and decided that she could trust him, should she need to. He clearly liked the animals more than

Ackerman or Darrell. She squirmed, signaling to be let down, and once Casper had set her back on the floor, she turned and ran to the space behind the bucket where she knew she could think quietly before making her next move. She had to get into Caruso's room before the operation, or maybe into the operating room, but either way she thought she would have to wait until it was time for Casper to move the calf. If all went well, Caruso could escape in the confusion she would create.

***

Ackerman stood before the students and explained the importance of the work they were about to do. His attention was briefly interrupted when he saw Casper at the back of the room leaning on the handle of a broom. He would soon fire the janitor who he considered useless. After all, it was twice in one day that he'd caught him not doing his job. As if understanding what Ackerman was thinking, Casper moved on, pushing his broom through the door and out into the hallway. He stood to one side of the door, hidden from the others in the room, to eavesdrop on what Ackerman was telling the students. He knew something was up and hoped he'd be able to find out what Ackerman was planning to do to the calf, and maybe to the cat too.

"We still haven't found the cat, but we must move on with our experiments. Tonight, we begin on the first experiment, and when we have finished, I will know valuable information about the animals we work with. I will share this information with you as we go along but remember that this is a secret project. You must not talk about the experiments with anyone outside of this group, and to make sure that you don't blab about our findings, I want all of you to sign this document."

Ackerman waved the forms in the air like he was conducting an orchestra, and then he handed them to Darrell to pass out to the other students.

"Once you have signed this form, you are not permitted to reveal the details of our work to anyone. Should you fail to do so, you will be fired immediately, and I will give the university a poor review of your performance."

The students looked up from the forms they held in their hands and exchanged nervous glances with each other. None of them had ever been threatened by an instructor, but the last thing they wanted was to receive a negative review. Each student signed their form and handed it back to Darrell. Then they waited to hear their instructions, even though they all hated both Ackerman and Darrell. Most hoped that one day both of them would be fired so a kinder person could take over the running of the research centre.

"All of you pay close attention to what I am about to say. I have evidence that Caruso can speak in our own language, and today we will remove his voice box. That will allow me to study it in detail, so I can determine what makes him different from the other animals. The voice box of the calf next door to him, a calf that doesn't speak, will be taken for comparison to help me determine what is allowing these animals to talk."

The students began to mutter amongst themselves, first because they thought he had lost his mind thinking that animals could speak like humans. Second, they all knew that the type of experiment he was going to do was against the rules for working with animals. Ackerman frowned and spoke again, more loudly this time, to get them back under his control.

"All of you be quiet, right now! How dare any of you lowly students question the ideas and decisions of a noted scientist like me. I have years of experience in animal research, and you are just beginners. When I give you an order, I expect you to jump to obey me, do you all understand?"

Casper, who still waited outside the room, heard Ackerman issuing orders like a bully. Like the students, he was shocked that the man really believed animals could speak. He also knew, even though he wasn't a scientist, that what Ackerman planned to do to the two calves was not only illegal, but cruel. Casper dropped his broom in the hallway and ran into the room to interrupt the scientist.

"You may think you're smarter than the rest of us, but you're also plain crazy, Ackerman. Everyone knows that animals can't talk like we humans do, and you're forgetting that these animals need their normal sounds to indicate their emotions, like fear and happiness. This type of experiment is cruel and it needs to be stopped, right now. It's not only ridiculous, but downright selfish to hurt an animal for such a stupid reason. We all know you're only doing this because you think you might get rich or famous if it works."

The students looked at Casper with wide eyes, completely stunned by his outburst because he was normally a very quiet man. Plus, no one ever criticized Ackerman and they feared the janitor would lose his job. Julia and Gerald, on the other hand, regretted that they didn't have Casper's courage because they both thought the same of Ackerman and his crazy idea.

"Casper, you are a simple-minded fool whose only talent is sweeping floors. Keep your silence and get back to your duties immediately or I will fire you."

Casper was not at all simple-minded. Although he was not formally educated like Ackerman, he knew more about the hearts and souls of animals than the scientist ever would. Casper's main problem was that he didn't know how he alone could stop Ackerman. He looked at the others in the room. There were six students who helped Ackerman with his experiments, and two animal workers who mainly did heavy jobs, like moving the animals from room to room. He couldn't tell who would be on his side if he tried to prevent the experiment on the two innocent little calves. He turned on his heel, left the room, and quickly headed down the hall, straight for the computer in the lunchroom. If he couldn't trust the people he worked with, he would get help from outside, and there wasn't a moment to lose.

Once seated at the computer, he looked up the phone numbers of groups related to animal welfare and phoned them all, even though it was well past office hours. With each call, he left an urgent message with details about what was going to happen. He didn't know if it would help, but at least he felt he had done something. Casper sighed and returned to the hall where he picked up his broom and returned to work. What he didn't know was that someone had indeed heard his complaints because all after hours calls to animal welfare agencies had been routed, under Max's orders, to his assistant, Sally Swan.

CHAPTER 16

Sally Swan

Sally Swan was twenty-five years old and getting rather bored with her job. She respected her boss Max but was tired of not being given important assignments in the field. After all, she had finished her training and had received high scores in both the written and physical parts of her final secret agent exams. She felt she could spy just as well as the other agents who were all men. In fact, she was a very athletic woman and had scored higher than all the men in the physical tests, whether it was scaling walls, long-distance running, or hand-to-hand combat. She wondered if Max thought of her as a daughter and wanted to protect her from the danger that came with many assignments. She would bring up the subject with him soon. He was a fair man, and she knew she could make him realize just how valuable she could be to his investigations.

Sally was sleeping when her cell phone rang. Her ring tone was a cardinal's song, and she woke instantly thinking the birds were already singing outside and it was time to get up. Her cat, Begonia, rose with disgust at being wakened, jumped from the bed to the floor, and then walked huffily out of the room. Her dog, Rusty, looked up and saw his chance to take Begonia's place on the bed. He jumped up eagerly, turned three times and then settled onto the eiderdown near Sally's feet. Rusty was a golden retriever with soft, brown eyes and a yellow coat that swished when there was a breeze. People often commented that his coat and Sally's hair were almost identical in colour and she would jokingly reply that owners begin to look more and more like their dogs over time.

It wasn't even midnight and Sally realized she'd only been asleep for an hour. She turned on the light and answered the phone. Someone named Casper had left a message and she listened to it. Her phone rang again and again, and she waited for it to stop before checking the rest of the messages. They were all from the same person about the research institute they were investigating, and she sat up in bed to make an urgent call to Max. He needed to know that there was indeed dangerous activity at the research centre that evening, and that there was someone on the inside who was prepared to help him take down Ackerman. When she finished her brief conversation with Max, she got out of bed and dressed to meet him at the research centre.

"He may not want me in the action, but this is the perfect opportunity for me to show him how good I am," she said to her dog.

Rusty barked in agreement because he knew his owner always wanted to help. Her energy never bothered him in the least. Like her, he wanted to be where the action was, and he jumped off the bed to follow her down the stairs to the kitchen. Sally gave Begonia some food and refreshed her water just in case they were gone longer than expected. Then she and Rusty ran to her car to head to the research centre. In the car, Rusty chewed on a dog biscuit while Sally ate a granola bar. She knew they would need that little bit of extra energy if they were to be of any help to Max.

Rusty looked out the window of the car after finishing his dog treat. He would have preferred some of the left-over roast beef that he knew was in the refrigerator, but assumed his owner understood his needs best. It was foggy again and he peered at the dark night beyond the passenger seat window, unable to make out the buildings they passed, even the ones he was familiar with. Instead of trying to see through the fog, Rusty stared at his reflection in the glass of the window and admired his beautiful coat. He had been blessed with a perfect retriever coat, and it didn't hurt that Sally brushed it regularly. Rusty had no idea where they were going, but suspected Sally was up to something dangerous and hoped it wouldn't be too risky. She was always trying new and often dangerous things, and that sometimes made him worry for her. At least she always takes me along though, he thought. If it wasn't for me, she'd be sure to get into some kind of trouble.

He turned to look at Sally and she told him what she knew about the research centre and Caruso the calf. She told him she didn't know very much about Max's special, secret spy apart from the fact that it was a cat named Cata Hari. Rusty wasn't particularly fond of cats because one had scratched his nose when he was only a puppy, when all he was trying to do was say hello to the creature. He had avoided them ever since, although he didn't mind Sally's cat, Begonia, even if she was a bit of a snob.

Sally went on to explain to Rusty that Max had never shared with her why the cat was so special and she joked that maybe the cat could talk or had a superpower like flying or becoming invisible. All Rusty knew was that they were headed to a research building on a mission to save innocent animals from an evil scientist. When Sally went on and on about how Max Wolf's secret spy would save the animals, Rusty snorted and turned away again because he'd heard enough about cats for one day. He just hoped that this one would be civilized.

CHAPTER 17

Cat and Mouse

Cata was curled up behind the bucket with her eyes closed while she thought about her plan. She was deep in thought about how she could ruin Ackerman's plans when she heard a squeaky voice say, "Hey, you can't be here. This is my spot!" Cata looked at the mouse, who spoke out of the side of his mouth while nibbling on a piece of food and debated whether to engage with it in conversation. This was the first talking rodent she had met, apart from the rabbit, Anilise, and she didn't know if he was trustworthy. Most cats saw mice as being far below their own level of intelligence. In fact, if she hadn't had work to do, she would have considered chasing it down the hall. Then she thought that she should be nice to the mouse because she was on her own and he might be useful to her mission.

"I'm sorry to be in the way, but I need to be here for my mission. I'm trying to save the animals from an evil scientist."

"Wow, you must be running for the cat of the year award or something. Most cats I know are mean, and extremely selfish. What's your name, Fur Ball?"

"Don't call me that. My name is Cata Hari, and I'm here to do important work. If you have nothing important to say, please leave me be so that I can think."

"Yeah, I get that all the time, how we rodents aren't important, we never actually do any good in the world, just destroy things and spread disease. Not all of us are like that you know. In fact, I pride myself on my cleanliness. Just the other day I was telling a friend of mine, a rat I know..."

"Stop blathering on about nothing. I'm working on a plan. You see I need to create a distraction so I can save one of the animals. Oh, I've just thought of a way for you to help, and you're going to help me whether you like it or not."

Cata thought the mouse had too much sass for politeness to work on him, so instead she bared her teeth. The mouse began to shake because he didn't want to become a bedtime snack anytime soon.

"Listen, I get it, this is important to you. I'll be happy to help you out, Cata Hari. I'm Jocko, by the way, and I busted out of one of those cages myself just last week. My buddies are still locked up, doing hard time behind bars."

"Thanks, Jocko. The animal who needs our help is a calf, and he's in that room over there. The scientist is going to operate on him in the room further down the hall. I don't have proof yet, but I think he's going to do something to the calf's voice. You see, he may have discovered that some of us animals can talk. After the operation, the calf, his name's Caruso, probably won't be able to sing anymore, and he has a rather lovely voice, if you like opera that is. It's a bigger problem than just one animal though, Jocko. Just imagine what would happen if the humans find out we animals can talk?"

"Whoa, that could be really bad. They already have enough power over us. I'll help you for sure, Cata Hari."

"Okay then, here's my plan. If you go into the operating room…"

"Oh yeah, I get it. It won't be sterile in there anymore if I go in."

"That's right, then I'll follow behind you and it'll be even less sterile, plus we might scare them too if the rest of my plan works. We have one human on our side here; his name is Casper. I saw him a little while ago and he looked very angry. I think he might punch the scientist, Ackerman, if he has a chance."

"Oh, not Ackerman, he's the worst. I believe that man was born under a rock. You know, I'm not even a lab mouse, I'm a field mouse. I swear I was just hanging out in the hall when that Dr. Ackerman saw me. He had one of his men put me in a cage. I don't know what happened to him to make him hate animals so much, but I bet his Mama wouldn't approve of what he does. It's like my friend Ernie, the groundhog, always says…"

"Jocko, no time for chit-chat because we need to focus now. We have important things to do," Cata said.

She explained her entire plan to the mouse and he agreed to do what she wanted. They had just finished discussing the plan when Cata heard footsteps.

"Shh, someone's coming. No one can know that we're here, Jocko, so make like a mouse and be quiet."

Jocko sighed, rolled his eyes at Cata, and said, "I can't believe you just said that to me, a mouse. Maybe from now on I will call you Fur Ball."

The footsteps moved closer and stopped outside Caruso's room. It was a young woman, and she shook her head in annoyance. She had clearly forgotten something and turned to go back to the operating room. Cata nodded to Jocko to let him know her plan was starting and he scurried as fast as he could, entering the operating room behind the heels of the technician. He hid behind one of the legs of a large table and settled in to wait until Cata was in position.

Cata remained in the hallway after Jocko had entered the operating room, because she thought she might be able to get information from other people passing by her hiding place. She knew Max needed her to get as much information about Ackerman as she could, and she was lucky that two other technicians stopped in the hall, not far from where she sat behind the bucket. They were discussing the procedure to be done on Caruso in detail and then went on to talk about how famous it would make Ackerman, although it was clear from the tone of their conversation that neither of them liked the scientist. Cata edged out a little from behind the bucket, just enough to direct the collar camera toward them. The camera had a microphone so that Max would be able to hear the plan on his laptop computer. She would wait there until it was no longer safe to do so. The most important thing, apart from her plan to ruin Ackerman's experiment on Caruso, was to make sure that Max knew what was going to happen.

The two women talked about how Ackerman did experiments that were banned years ago. Then they began talking about Caruso, and Cata cringed when she heard what Ackerman planned to do to the poor calf. She was thinking how much she wanted to ruin Ackerman's plan when the conversation turned to a discussion of her. Ackerman planned to operate on "the pesky cat" once she was caught. When the technicians moved toward the operating room, Cata followed ever so quietly behind them. She crept into the room and fled immediately to a corner where the light was dim and she wouldn't be seen by any of the workers. She saw Jocko in his position near the table where they would operate on Caruso, and she winked at him. The room was quiet, with only the whispered conversation between the workers, but then Cata heard a voice outside loudly shouting orders and she knew that Ackerman was on his way.

CHAPTER 18

Emma and Mustafa Take the Lead

Emma woke up not long after falling asleep. She looked to her right and did not see Smokey where she would usually be, curled up and sleeping near her pillow. She got out of bed and looked around the room and then in the closet. Bending down, she peeked under the bed, but there was no sign of her cat. She wasn't sure what to do, maybe wake her parents? No, she thought, they would not like that at all. Emma didn't know where her cat was, but she had a bad feeling she could not explain. She began to search the room again, calling softly for Smokey.

Mustafa was sleeping in his usual spot between the front door and the foot of the stairs. He woke abruptly and looked about, sensing danger. He knew Cata was in trouble, but he could also feel in his bones that something was wrong in his house. He ran upstairs as quietly as he could and peeked into the master bedroom. Both people were safe and sleeping soundly, the man snoring softly. He moved to Emma's room and there he discovered the reason that he felt unsettled about his pack. Emma was out of bed and frantically searching for something. Mustafa moved closer to let her feel his protection.

"Oh Mustafa, I can't find Smokey and she always sleeps here. She never explores the house at night and I don't know what to do. Do you know where she is?"

Emma was surprised when Mustafa seemed to nod his head in response to her question, and she knelt to look in the dog's eyes. He always seemed so wise, almost like he was watching over them to keep them from making mistakes. Mustafa was already fearful that something bad was about to happen to Cata, and knowing he needed human help this time, he decided to take the cat's earlier advice. Emma was indeed a very smart girl and he would get her to help him. He took her wrist gently in his mouth and pulled her toward the door.

"Something's wrong, isn't it, Mustafa? You want me to go with you? I know that you sense things we humans can't, just like you did with the break-in. I wish you could talk so you could tell me all about it. I'll come with you but let me change out of my pajamas first."

Emma dressed quickly and then followed Mustafa out of her bedroom. She knew she had to avoid one step in the staircase, the one that always squeaked. Her worry was for nothing though because all she had to do was follow the dog's path. He seemed to know how to avoid the squeaky spot, and she wondered what else this smart dog of theirs seemed to know. She unlocked the front door quietly and opened it slowly, so as not to wake her parents. Then she and Mustafa were outside, down the steps, through the front gate, and running down the street.

***

Max had grown concerned about Cata because the only image he saw on his computer screen for many minutes was a bucket. He knew she sometimes had a cat nap on missions but wasn't sure if it was that or if she was hiding from danger. He debated going in to help her, but he needed to see evidence of Ackerman doing something wrong before rushing in. He decided to wait until the agreed upon check in time with the cat before making a move. He looked at his watch and saw that there were still ninety minutes to wait.

"Why do the minutes always pass so slowly at times like this?" he said.

When he looked back at the screen, he saw movement. Were his eyes playing tricks on him, or was that a mouse nodding before scurrying away? Moments later, the camera picked up an image of workers and he could hear their conversation. Cata was feeding him information about the operation on the calf and he was filled with awe at the cat's intelligence and bravery. He became alarmed when the workers began talking about a cat. Then the scene changed on his computer screen, and he could see that Cata was on the move, running toward danger.

***

"Mustafa, where are we going? I've never been this way before, and never so far from home on my own. Mom and Dad will be mad enough that I'm not in bed, but when they discover that I've gone outside at night, they'll probably ground me for a whole year."

Mustafa stopped and barked softly at Emma and then took hold of her arm softly in his mouth again, dragging her gently to get her to follow.

"Okay, okay, already. We'd better get where we're going soon though."

The young girl followed the dog, increasing her pace behind Mustafa when he started to run. He slowed from time to time to look behind him and make sure she was keeping up. They ran through the dark, foggy streets until a large building appeared before them.

"What is this place, Mustafa? Darn, I wish you could talk."

Mustafa barked and began running full speed toward the building just as Max was getting out of his car. He was spun around, first by the dog, and then a second time by the girl, who said, "Oops! Sorry, Mister!" as she went. He didn't know who the dog and girl were and was afraid they would spoil the mission. He put his laptop computer under his arm and followed them to the back of the building. The electric door at the loading dock hadn't closed completely, leaving just enough room for the little girl and dog to get inside. He realized he had no choice but go in too, and if he couldn't squeeze through the small space, he'd have to find another way in. He couldn't let a child be exposed to Ackerman.

CHAPTER 19

Cata's Secret is Revealed

Cata heard noises in the hall and knew Caruso was being moved. After all, his loud mooing was hard to mistake. If she didn't act soon, he'd be put to sleep for the operation. Ackerman and his assistants were wearing gowns, masks, surgical gloves, and even booties on their feet. Just as Cata was preparing to make her move, Ackerman started yelling orders.

"Make sure you're all mentally prepared for this and give me room to work. When I ask for an instrument, I want it in my hand within seconds, do you all understand me? If anything goes wrong or if anyone makes a mistake, no matter how small, you'll be given a bad review. That should give you enough incentive to perform your jobs properly."

Gerald Otterman stood behind Ackerman to observe the surgery. He rolled his eyes at Julia, and even though they wore surgical masks, he could tell she had smiled by the light in her eyes. They had both spoken with Casper earlier and knew he had called the authorities, but they were afraid help might be too late for Caruso, and for the cat, wherever she was. They could only hope that help would arrive soon and Ackerman would be stopped before the operation on the poor calf. They also hoped that a kinder person would take over the running of the research institute. They both looked at each other with alarm when Caruso's mooing became louder. They could hear the poor calf kicking against the sides of his cart as he was being moved closer to the operating room.

While Gerald and Julia were exchanging looks, Cata was watching Jocko, and was amused when the mouse tried to roll his eyes just like one of Ackerman's workers had. Then he made circles beside his head with his paw to say Ackerman was crazy. Cata agreed and winked at him, but their fun stopped when the wheels of Caruso's cart banged against the outside of the door. The animal workers' shouts could be heard as the door opened and Caruso was wheeled into the room. The calf looked terrified and bucked against the sides of the cart. Cata motioned with her paw to Jocko, and he emerged from behind the table leg to position himself near the shoe of Darrell Krump. Moments later Cata's plan began.

"Aieeee! There's something on my foot! Oh no, it's running up my leg."

Darrell was frantic and shook his leg wildly. When that didn't work, he began running around the room, stopping every few seconds to shake his leg again. Ackerman was yelling, trying to be heard above both Darrell's screams and Caruso's mooing. Casper Fox chose that moment to run into the room to beg Ackerman to stop the procedure.

"You get out of my operating room right now, Casper Fox. As of now, you're fired, so just leave the building. Better yet, you there, managing the cart, escort him from the building now. I don't want to see you on the premises again, Fox, and if you do come back, I'll call the police. For goodness sake Darrell, stop your childishness and help with the calf. All of you, let's get moving..."

Ackerman never had a chance to finish his sentence, and the others were shocked silent because something shot through the air and landed on the scientist's face. It was Cata, who had moved into position during the confusion and hurled herself at the man.

"Oh, get this thing off me. Owww!"

Cata had intentionally scratched the man in hopes that the experiment on Caruso would be stopped. The animal workers, who had been ordered to remove Casper from the building, decided they were tired of being told what to do and began to laugh at Ackerman's struggle with the cat. Cata chose that moment to jump from Ackerman's head onto the table. That was when Julia saw the chance to scatter the sterile surgical tools to the floor, so the surgery couldn't be performed. Cata saw the look of anger on Ackerman's face and she wasted no time running from the room before he could catch her, and Jocko followed close behind. She could hear more shouts from Ackerman as she left though, and she realized her job was not yet over.

"Sterilize more equipment now. I want this calf dealt with tonight, and somebody get that blasted cat! I want it in a cage now. Oh, what am I saying! I'll do it myself. I always have to do it myself or nothing ever gets done around here!"

Ackerman ran into the hallway, and he was much faster than Cata had expected. She was almost at the loading dock, so close to escape, when Ackerman grabbed her unkindly by the tail, swinging her back and forth for all to see. She struggled to reach up to claw the man, but he was swinging her too fast for her to manage it. Instead she meowed and hissed as loudly as she could. Ackerman knew it was the cat he'd seen on the security tape, and the same one he'd tried to have kidnapped earlier in the week. He wondered why it wasn't talking. Maybe I was wrong, he thought. He decided that even if it couldn't talk, it was still a menace and he needed to do something about it.

"I have an idea for this cat, but it will have to wait until we finish with Caruso. You there, put this animal in a cage and then get back here on the double."

"Sure, Dr. Ackerman, straight away," Gerald Otterman said.

Gerald continued down the hall, holding Cata tightly in his arms, but he had no plan of putting the cat in a cage. Instead he signaled to Casper who was still in the hallway, and the older man joined him when Ackerman had returned to the operating room. Cata didn't know Gerald, and she didn't trust him, so she squirmed in his arms and jumped toward Casper. He caught her, petted her head, and gently rubbed the side of her face.

"Settle down, little one. You can trust Gerald here. He hates Ackerman as much as I do."

He loosened his grip on Cata, and she jumped down to the floor and turned to face the two men.

"My name is Cata Hari, and I need your help. I think Ackerman's going to remove Caruso's voice box, and the calf wants to be an opera singer. Can you help me stop him?"

Gerald went pale and fainted to the floor as soon as the cat spoke. Casper's mouth formed a perfect O and he jumped away from the cat. He put one hand on the wall of the hallway and the other on his chest as he breathed deeply to recover from his shock at hearing the cat speak. Then he scratched his head and looked down at the cat.

"Am I dreaming? Did you just talk?"

"I don't have time to answer your questions right now, Casper. It's a long story, and I'll fill you in later, but right now we must focus on the problem at hand. Dr. Ackerman is doing bad things to the animals here, and I have evidence on my collar camera to show to the authorities. But right now, Caruso is in danger. He's too big for me to help on my own and, as you just saw, Dr. Ackerman tried to put me in a cage. My friend Mustafa will be here soon to help me, but right now I need human help."

Casper was about to answer when he saw a dog and a little girl running toward him and the cat. The little girl was yelling Smokey, and the dog, who was very large, was growling low in his throat. Casper backed against the wall again and moved a transport cart in front of him.

"That's okay Casper, he won't hurt you. They're both with me. This is Mustafa and my dear Emma," Cata said.

"Smokey, you can talk?" Emma asked.

"Smokey? Her name is Cata Hari, she just told me." Casper said.

"She's my cat, and her name is Smokey. Look at your fur, Smokey, you need a good brushing. Wait a second, how long have you been able to talk?" Emma asked with her hands on her hips.

"I'll explain later, sweet Emma, but it's most important that you promise to keep my secret, you too Casper. Animal speech is not something the world is ready to know about. Emma, use your cell phone to call the following number. Ask for Max and tell him I've cracked the case. Tell him that we need the police here right away."

Emma was full of questions but put them aside. Instead, she punched in the number as Cata recited it to her, and the call was answered after only one ring. With all the excitement of the talking cat, and the arrival of the girl and dog, Casper forgot to keep an eye out for trouble. Had he been more careful, he would have seen that someone else was in the hallway and was listening in on their conversation. It was Darrell, and when the group moved with Cata toward the loading dock to meet up with Max, he ran in the other direction, to the operating room, to warn Ackerman.

CHAPTER 20

A Little Help from her Friends

When Sally Swan arrived at the research building, she saw Max trying to lift the loading dock door with difficulty. She parked her car and she and Rusty ran toward him.

"Max, I was worried about you. I had a terrible feeling that you were in trouble and needed help. What can we do?"

"Thank you Sally, but you and Rusty should go home. It may be too dangerous for you to be here," Max said.

Sally reached down to try to help him lift the door. It wasn't the best time for it, but she decided to convince him that she would make an excellent agent, if only he'd give her a chance.

"Oh, come on Max, you said I could start going on missions with you. You know I don't have enough work to keep me busy in the office all day. I took the advanced training course in espionage, and I got almost a perfect score on the exam. I got the highest mark in the class."

"Well, okay Sally, maybe I have been too protective of you. I guess it is time you got your feet wet but be careful to follow my orders when we're in there. Ackerman may have once been a respected scientist, but something happened to him along the way. If he can do bad things to animals, he can certainly do the same to people."

"I promise I'll follow orders, Max," Sally said. Rusty woofed his agreement.

Before they could get the door raised, Max's phone rang and he was surprised to hear a child's voice at the other end. He put the girl on speaker so that Sally could listen. When he realized Cata and the others were in danger, and likely out-numbered, Max phoned for help from his back-up agents. While he made the call, the loading dock door opened from the inside and he found Casper and a still groggy Gerald waiting.

"Let's do names later. I'm Cata Hari's boss, and I know she's in trouble or she wouldn't have sent a message to me."

"We need as much help as we can get," Casper said. "Most of the workers here are on our side, but Ackerman's sidekick, Darrell Krump, told Ackerman that we saved Cata from being put in a cage. Ackerman just caught Cata again and he's threatening to do something awful to her this time."

"Where are they?"

"Follow us."

Casper and Gerald were joined by Julia, and the three led Max, Sally, and Rusty to the bottom of a high staircase where Mustafa and

Emma were staring upward. At the top, Ackerman was holding Cata by the tail again, but this time she was swinging ten feet or more above the ground. She struggled to get free, but Ackerman wasn't making it easy for her. Cata was so frightened that she had forgotten how to use her words, and instead only meowed. Mustafa knew she was terrified that the man would let her drop to the floor below, and he wanted to reassure her. He didn't want any of the humans to find out about his speech, so he spoke in the softest whisper to the cat, one he thought only another animal would hear.

"Don't worry, Cata, if he drops you, I'll break your fall. I'll never let anything happen to you," he said.

But Gerald had very acute hearing and looked to see where the whisper came from. When he realized that another animal was speaking, he fainted again. Before anyone could help him, all attention was suddenly taken up by a high-pitched, squeaky voice that seemed to come from nowhere.

"Hang in there, Fur Ball!"

The animal workers looked around but couldn't identify the speaker. Meanwhile, Casper and Max, who were concentrating only on Cata, ran up the stairs. They had to get to Ackerman in order to save her, and both were determined that it would be the last time the man would ever touch an animal. Max charged at the scientist while Casper snatched Cata from his hands. Cata was shaking with fear and he held her tightly to soothe her fright. Casper was about to let Cata down to the ground so that he could help Max when Mustafa raced up the stairs. He chomped down hard on Ackerman's ankle and refused to let go. Neither Max nor Mustafa released their holds on the scientist until help arrived.

Max's agents and the police broke through the front door of the building and quickly placed Ackerman in handcuffs. At the urging of the other workers, Darrell was taken into custody as well, and both he and the scientist were led out the door to a waiting police car. The students talked amongst themselves excitedly because they had so many questions. Was Caruso all right? What would happen to the animals now? What would happen to Ackerman and Darrell?

Max kept control of things and asked the workers to get back to their jobs. He wanted to be sure that all the animals were safe and had enough food and water for the night. He knew the animal welfare authorities would arrive in the morning to check on all of them. He was most concerned about Caruso and he asked Cata, Sally, and Casper to join him when he checked on the calf. They found him still in the transport cart which had been moved back into the hall. He had stopped bucking and shaking and was humming to himself.

"Caruso, we're so glad you're safe. They're going to take you back to your stall for the night, and I promise nothing else will happen to you. Dr. Ackerman has been taken away by the police," Cata said.

"That was a close one all right. Thank you, Cata, you really saved my hide."

Max and Sally laughed at the calf who could still find humor after his horrible experience. Max learned from Caruso the name of the farmer he was stolen from and called him, despite the late hour. When he hung up, he had good news for Caruso.

"You and your friends are going home soon, Caruso. Your farmer will be here in the morning to pick you up."

"Oh, thank you so much, but could you take me back to my stall now? It's rather chilly in this hall and the draft from the loading dock can't be good for my voice."

Julia and a still groggy Gerald had joined them and they helped Casper wheel Caruso back to his room and then led him into his stall. With order restored, the animals checked on and fed, and the police taking charge of the building, Max told the others that it was time to leave. Sally went back home with Rusty to make them a special meal, and to make sure that Begonia was all right. Max drove Cata, Mustafa, and Emma home, and the three sneaked quietly back into the house so as not to wake the Barrett's. Emma kissed Mustafa and he laid down near the stairs, ready to protect his pack if necessary. Emma changed, settled back into bed, and let Smokey's purrs lull her to sleep. There would be time for questions and answers the following day.

CHAPTER 21

Lunch in the Park

George and Candace Barrett remained in the dark about the exploits of Emma, Mustafa, and especially Smokey. Emma had agreed with Smokey that it would be best if no one else knew that she, or any other animal, could talk. Emma carried on as usual, studying and going to school, walking Mustafa when she returned home, and playing with Smokey afterward. She would no longer worry when her cat sometimes mysteriously disappeared, and she would not fret when the cat seemed overly tired.

Two weeks after Ackerman's arrest on charges that included cruelty to animals, Cata waited for Max at their regular meeting place in the park. As she lay in the cool grass beneath the picnic table she wondered if Max had another important mission for her. She hoped that if he did, it would not involve animals in cages or evil scientists. She was a sensitive cat and what had happened to the poor animals at the hands of Ackerman and Darrell had upset her more than she let on. She was thinking about what would eventually happen to those two when she heard the unmistakeable voice of Jocko.

"Hey, Cata Hari, how're you doing?"

"I expected you to say Fur Ball. I'm doing much better now than when I last saw you. How about you, Jocko? What are you up to?"

"Well, I tried to free the other mice, but I couldn't get anywhere with the locks on their cages. I overheard one of the workers say that the mice hadn't been used in experiments yet and would probably be sent to another research place. Too bad I couldn't free them, but I tried my best. Since then I met a nice, lady field mouse. We're thinking about traveling down south where it's warmer and the living is easier. My friend, the groundhog, told me about a place down there where there's enough food on the street to keep me and my lady friend nice and chubby. My other friend, the rat I told you about..."

"Jocko, you do go on and on, don't you? You could get a job in politics from what I hear the humans at home say."

"It's true, I do chat quite a lot, but you must agree that everything I utter is pure gold. Anyway, say hello to your friend Max for me. He seemed like a nice guy, for a human. I'm off to meet Daisy, my lady friend, for our big trip. Take care of yourself, Fur Ball."

"You take care too, Jocko. Enjoy the warm weather."

Jocko scampered away and Cata sniffed the air. She could smell fish and chips and, knowing Max couldn't be too far away, she jumped onto the seat of the picnic table. Max didn't keep her waiting long, but when he sat down on the seat beside her, he kept the fish away from her.

"I'm really hungry, Max. May I please have some fish?"

"We have to wait for the others, Cata."

"What others? This is our secret meeting place so there can't be others."

Cata was unhappy that Max would let anyone come to their secret place, but her mood improved when she heard a familiar voice and realized that Max had invited Emma to join them. She had forgotten it was a Saturday and the little girl had the day off from school. Emma ran toward them with Mustafa on a leash. From another direction came Casper, Julia, and Gerald, with Sally Swan and Rusty bringing up the rear.

"They all know your secret now Cata, and they know you're my agent. By the way, we have one new agent starting today. I've recruited Casper to enter the program and he'll be around to help you in the future. Of course, Sally is one of our best agents, and you will be working with her on missions too. Then there's Gerald, who has agreed to be our new scientific advisor when he's finished university. Sorry we couldn't let you do the agent training Gerald, but you faint a little too often for that."

"I understand Max, and besides, I don't think I'm cut out to be a spy. Both Casper and I are happy to have this new chance though and be far away from Ackerman."

"What about Julia? Is she an agent too?" Emma asked.

"No, I'll be finishing my university program soon, just in time to start my new courses. You see, I just found out I've been accepted into veterinary school."

"That's wonderful, Julia. Now enough with you grown-ups, what about Emma? Mustafa and Rusty helped too. What about them?" Cata asked.

"I thought it would be nice to make them honorary agents since they showed such bravery in helping us on the mission. Maybe Mustafa would like to become a full-time agent since he already helps you out on missions from time to time. It's okay Mustafa, I heard you whisper to Cata, so did Casper and Gerald. We know you can talk. Would you like to join us?"

Mustafa had been listening all along but was pretending to be a non-talking dog by looking bored with the conversation and watching a butterfly flutter nearby instead. When he heard what Max said about him though, he looked first from Max to Casper, and then from Emma to Cata. Cata shook her head at him, but then gave what seemed to be a shrug, at least as close to a shrug as a cat can get. The dog nodded at Cata and turned to face Max.

"That's very thoughtful of you Max, but no thank you, I can't accept your offer. I have enough to do protecting my own pack, you see," the German shepherd replied.

Emma gazed at her dog, stunned. She had not heard Mustafa speak at the research centre so she was completely surprised when Max had asked the dog a question and expected an answer. Hearing Mustafa reply made her wonder what else he and Smokey had been keeping from her.

Before she could dwell on it any longer though, Max began opening the packages of food with Sally's help. He had brought enough for a real feast. Soon they were enjoying their meal and talking about the future. Sally was happy that Max had decided to let her go on missions, but she was still amazed that Cata, Mustafa, and Caruso could talk, because her own dog had never uttered a peep.

"Talking animals, who would have thought it possible?" she asked.

"It helps us to keep you humans safe," Mustafa said.

Rusty nodded and said, "Yeah, tell me about it. They'd never survive without us."

Sally looked at her dog and her mouth formed a perfect O in surprise, while Gerald surprised no one by fainting.

ABOUT THE AUTHOR

KAREN COPELAND is a PhD scientist who draws on her own experience in research in writing fiction. She is the author of the Ottawa Valley Mysteries series. She lives in Ottawa, Canada.

Contact her at https://karencopeland.wordpress.com.